LETTER NUMBER TWO

"Oh, I almost forgot." Sam rummaged in his jacket pocket and drew out a wrinkled letter. "This was in the Incoming Heart-to-Heart box. I heard the box lid creak open while I was looking in my files, but I didn't see who put it in there. I thought you'd like to see it. It's marked TOP SECRET."

"Thanks." As Virginia took the letter, a shiver of apprehension rippled through her. She stepped into the light on her porch and ripped open Desperate's envelope.

> Dear Heart,
> Ding-dong the witch is dead. Now she calls the grave her bed. She did us all a favor. Happy?

"Oh, my god," Virginia moaned, dropping the letter as if it were on fire. "This person is a total sicko."

Look for all of Jahnna N. Malcolm's thrillers

Leo: Stage Fright
Virgo: Desperately Yours
Libra: Into the Light
Scorpio: Death Grip

Available from HarperPaperbacks

Virgo

DESPERATELY YOURS

by

Jahnna N. Malcolm

HarperPaperbacks
A Division of HarperCollinsPublishers

This is a work of fiction. The characters, incidents, and dialogues are products of the author's imagination and are not to be construed as real. Any resemblance to actual events or persons, living or dead, is entirely coincidental.

HarperPaperbacks *A Division of* HarperCollins*Publishers*
10 East 53rd Street, New York, N.Y. 10022

Copyright © 1995 by Malcolm Hillgartner and Jahnna Beecham

Cover illustration by Danilo Ducak

First printing: August 1995

Printed in the United States of America

HarperPaperbacks and colophon are trademarks of HarperCollins*Publishers*

❖ 10 9 8 7 6 5 4 3 2 1

For Laura Young and Trevor Young Marston

DESPERATELY YOURS

chapter 1

VIRGO (August 23–September 22)—
Neptune will be puzzling you for some time
this week. Stay on your toes! Your ever-logical
mind tends to get snagged in the details and
miss the Big Picture. No matter how you slice
it, there may be a grave misunderstanding here.

"When is this going to end? Will you ever stop
torturing me?"

The raspy voice came from inside a small
wooden outbuilding behind Fairview High.

Virginia Wells stood frozen in place, listening.
It was not even eight o'clock in the morning.
School didn't start for another forty-five min-
utes. *Who would be in the newsroom at this hour?*

"That's it! I'm outta here."

Crash.

*My god. Whoever's in there is destroying the news-
paper office.* My *newspaper!* Virginia sprang forward. The door swung open just before she
reached it.

"Leave me alone. I mean it!" A girl with dark hair pulled back into a tight ponytail stumbled out onto the snow-covered grass. The cardboard box she was carrying flew out of her arms and skidded across the icy ground.

"Kim?" Virginia hurried to help her friend.

"Oh, God." Kim's face was red and her hands shook as she tried to pick up the items that had tumbled out of the box.

Virginia couldn't believe her eyes. Kim Keller, one of the most attractive girls in all of Fairview High, was barely recognizable. Her eyes were puffy and red from crying. Mascara stained her cheeks. She wasn't wearing a jacket, and it was freezing cold outside. "Kim, are you okay?"

Kim, who was on her knees scrambling to collect her belongings, flinched as she saw Virginia for the first time. "No. I'm not okay."

"Here, let me help you." Virginia carefully stacked her notebook and files on the ground next to her purse, then bent to help Kim. She picked up an ankle bracelet with a dangling heart charm.

"Give me that!" Kim yanked the bracelet out of Virginia's hand and tossed it in the box. "Don't help me, Virginia. I can do it myself."

Kim scooped the remaining items into the box, looking nervously over her shoulder at the little building they called the Bungalow.

Virginia followed her gaze. "Kim? What's going on? Who were you fighting with?"

Kim stood up, clutching the box tightly to her chest. "Look, Virginia, I don't want to talk about it. Forget you saw me."

Kim made a move for the parking lot, and Virginia grabbed her arm. Her skin felt cold and clammy. "Kim, I don't know what's going on with you, but you can't leave."

"What do you mean, I can't?" Kim's big brown eyes looked overbright with fear. "I've got to."

"Don't you remember what day this is?"

Kim just stared in response.

"It's Friday, the last day of January," Virginia said, hoping Kim would get a clue. "The *Spectator* is due at three-thirty today." She checked her watch. "We have exactly seven hours to finish paste-up and get the edited copy to the printer."

Kim looked over her shoulder one more time. "I really don't care about that, Ginny," she said in a low, earnest voice. "Please just let me get to my car and get out of here."

Virginia blinked at her friend in amazement.

Kim really looked scared. In all the years that she had known Kim, nothing had fazed her. In Girl Scouts, when everyone else was afraid to go near the river's edge at Lyon Park, Kim would be there, wading through the murky water, her uniform soaked from hem to waist. On Halloween, in the seventh grade, she was the first one into the deserted old Heifner house. And when they reached high school, she was the first to challenge an unjust rule or champion a worthy cause. Kim had been fearless. Until now.

"Look, Kim, I don't know what's frightened you, but maybe you should go inside and get warm. Take a few deep breaths before you go anywhere."

"I don't have time," Kim shouted. "I just need to leave."

Kim's shout startled Virginia, and she heard herself shouting back, "You can't leave. We're on a really tight deadline. I'm counting on you to help get the paper in. *Everyone's* counting on you."

Kim's face twisted into an angry grimace. "God, Virginia, would you just lay off? You're so afraid you'll lose your position as editor that you don't care about anyone or anything but your stupid deadlines. Well, get this—I don't care about deadlines."

"You used to care," Virginia charged. "Is it because Ms. Burns didn't choose you to be in the finals for editor next term?"

Every semester the position of editor of the *Spectator* was up for grabs. The whole staff had applied before Christmas and recently their adviser, Ms. Burns, had narrowed the field to four: Jo Plunkett, Emily Wolfe, Sam Calhoun, and Virginia. It had caused an enormous amount of tension amoung all of them. But Kim had seemed to take the news just fine. If that's what had her upset now, this would be a major delayed reaction.

"Virginia—" Kim's chin began to quiver and she fought hard to keep from crying. "Some things are more important in life than getting chosen to be editor of this dinky school's paper. But you wouldn't understand that. You never have problems. Because you are Miss Perfect."

Ow! That stung. Virginia backed away from Kim and picked up her notebook and files. "Well, if that's the way you feel . . ."

Kim saw the hurt look on Virginia's face and flung her head back. "Oh, God, Ginny."

Thunk!

The door of the Bungalow slammed shut behind them and Kim jumped so high she nearly dropped her box again. Both girls turned to look at the Bungalow door. No one came out. That meant someone must have gone in.

Shoot. Now I'll never know who Kim was arguing with.

When Virginia turned back to look at Kim, she was already running toward the parking lot, leaving Virginia to try to get the *Spectator* in on time practically by herself.

"My deadline! What am I supposed to do?" Virginia called after her. The school yard was starting to fill up and several students passing by on the quad shot her looks that said, "Major Weirdo."

Virginia didn't care. She was used to it. Somewhere around junior high, the kids in school had seemed to split into two categories. There were those who were very social, but academic washouts—and there were the overachievers—those who studied, got good grades, and cared about school. Virginia fell into the second category. Unfortunately, in that category, social life was seriously lacking.

Virginia carefully checked her papers to make sure the snow hadn't gotten on them, which made her remember Kim's column; Heart-to-Heart. *I'm not going to get stuck with that. That's her job.*

Virginia jogged after Kim, trying to catch her before she reached her car.

"What about the Heart-to-Heart letters?" Virginia demanded, grabbing Kim's arm once again. "You can't leave until you turn those letters in."

Kim, who was struggling to unlock the door of a beat-up red Toyota, rolled her eyes. "God, Virginia. Don't you ever let up?"

"No," Virginia answered, stiffly. "That's the editor's job. To keep on top of her staff."

Kim fumbled for her notebook, which was sticking out of the cardboard box, and yanked out a piece of paper. "Here."

Virginia stared at the paper.

Dear Heart,

I got a lousy grade on my chemistry exam and I'm sure it's because Mr. Schwartz doesn't like me. He's always calling on me when I don't know the answers. What should I do?

Stumped

Beneath the letter, scrawled in Kim's handwriting, was her reply.

Dear Stumped,
  Study.

"This is it?" Virginia waved the letter in Kim's face. "I can't print this."

"Then toss it. Just leave me alone."

Kim climbed behind the steering wheel and started the engine.

"When are you coming back?" Virginia shouted to Kim as she backed out of her parking spot.

"I don't know," Kim screamed. "Later!"

With tires squealing, Kim's car careened out of the parking lot, Virginia stood on the cement divider, watching until the little red car disappeared into the swirling gray fog.

What a totally bizarre morning. First the shouting match in the *Spectator* Bungalow, then Kim's weird behavior. *What's going to happen next?*

As if in reply, a second set of tires squealed out of the parking lot. Virginia turned quickly. Whoever it was vanished into the heavy mist right behind Kim. Why would so many students be leaving school? *What's going on, anyway?*

A gust of cold wind blew a strand of Virginia's shoulder-length brown hair across her face. Normally she wore it in a French braid, but today she'd worn it loose. *Big mistake.* In this wind, her fine hair was going every which way.

"Virginia!" Ms. Burns, the newspaper adviser, called to her from the school's back door. "I have an ad in my office that has to make this edition. Could you come pick it up?"

Virginia glanced back at the Bungalow. By now, several students had come and gone. Who had Kim been talking to? And why had she sounded and acted so frightened?

"Virginia?"

"Coming." She pushed thoughts of Kim from her mind as she hurried to Ms. Burns's office, located just inside the back door of the science wing. The tall, sandy-haired adviser frowned at her from beside her cluttered desk. "Is the issue almost ready? You only have till three-thirty, you know."

"I know. It'll be ready."

If I skip my classes, act like a jerk to the rest of the staff, get an ulcer, and develop superhuman typing skills between now and then.

Ms. Burns smiled. "Good."

Virginia took the ad from Ms. Burns and headed once again out the back door of the school. Kim's face flashed through her mind. She'd been frightened. There was no other explanation for the way she had acted.

Frightened. But of what?

chapter 2

Neat and orderly, you expect those around you to be the same. Watch this obsession. A little chaos now and then is all right, Virgo. Try not to be too critical. Not everyone has the scientific mind you have. Brace yourself for an unexpected surprise. By week's end, you gain new insight into a difficult problem.

"Emily made a mistake." Virginia uncapped her red pen and corrected the spelling error. "I hope it's not bad luck to change a horoscope." *Especially my own.*

It was one-thirty Friday afternoon and Virginia was ready to scream. With an hour till deadline, they were two articles short, and Casey Collier, the staff photographer, still hadn't brought in her photos of the Moonlight Madness Dance.

"Jo, would you remind me to tell Emily to proof her work?"

Jo Plunkett, the assistant editor, sat at her computer terminal against the far wall, her short spiky hair sticking out like a scrub brush gone haywire. Her funky paisley vest hung half off her shoulder. "If I were you, I wouldn't touch that horoscope," she said, leaning back in her metal folding chair. "Emily is sooo picky about it. It's always precise to the last millimeter."

"Well, if she's so picky about it—where is she?" Virginia snapped, throwing her hands in the air. "Where's my staff?"

"Beats me," Jo replied. "I saw Trip at lunch, and Emily was here just a little while ago. But I haven't seen Kim all day."

Kim! A tight, heavy knot of tension coiled in Virginia's stomach. *Should I mention the exchange I had with Kim? How scared she looked? Or will Jo think I'm exaggerating?*

"I saw her early this morning, coming out of the Bungalow," Virginia said, carefully. "She seemed pretty upset."

"What about?" Jo asked, crossing to the printer.

"I'm not sure." Virginia studied Jo's face. Maybe she was the person Kim had been fighting with. "But Kim had definitely been crying. She carried a huge cardboard box to her car and drove out of the parking lot like a maniac, saying she'd be back later. But so far, no Kim.

It all seemed to be news to Jo, who tore off the printed article and handed it to Virginia. "That's Kim. She's been so moody lately."

Virginia studied the article Jo had given her. It was the sports feature. She read the headline out loud. "'Fairview Team Wins Game.'" Virginia shook her head in frustration. "Come on, Jo, this headline won't do. Kill it."

"Kill it?" Jo made a sour face. "Why?"

"It's boring." Virginia handed it back to Jo, then grabbed the electric waxer and pasted the last two ads along one edge of the newspaper. "You know what Ms. Burns says: Headlines make the paper."

"Oh, puh-leeze." Jo tugged at her hair, which only made it stand up even straighter in the air. "Sports headlines are always so corny. What do you want me to say? 'Grizzlies Bite Cougars'? 'Grizzlies Crunch Cougars'?"

"Well . . . yes." Virginia pushed her bangs out of her eyes with her free hand. "Those will do for starters. They're much more catchy."

Jo blew her lips out in frustration. "Okay! You're the boss."

Her words had an extra edge. Ever since Ms. Burns had made her announcement about

the finalists for editor, Jo had been tense.
Which was pretty silly, since she was one of the
finalists.

Jo made a big show of slamming her chair
around as she positioned herself in front of her
keyboard. While she typed, she muttered, "Kill
the Cougars. Cream the Cougars. Crunch the
Cougars."

Virginia grabbed the waxer, which was a
device shaped like a paint roller, and vented her
frustration on the ad page. *Slide. Stick. Ick.* This
competition was ruining everything. The finalists were uptight, and the ones not chosen were
resentful and angry. *Slide. Stick. Ick.* Not a great
recipe for staff teamwork.

The door to the newsroom burst open and
Trip McFadden, staff artist and resident cynic,
cruised in, his high-top sneakers squeaking on
the floor. "Everyone can relax. I'm here."

Virginia smiled at him. Trip was so skinny he
looked like a parenthesis. He had broad shoulders and moved with a catlike grace she'd always
kind of liked. He was wearing his usual jeans and
T-shirt with the motto CUM DIGNITATE OTIUM
(*LEISURE WITH DIGNITY*) written across it. She shook
her head. How could someone so laid-back

produce such dark, sarcastic, and ruthlessly funny illustrations?

"Anybody see Kim?" he asked, tossing his weather-beaten parka and books on his chair by the art table. "We were supposed to meet at lunch to go over that article on the choir concert." He looked at Jo, then back to Virginia. "She didn't show up."

"Virginia said she left school this morning," Jo said, gesturing at Virginia with her thumb.

Trip cocked his head, focusing his pale blue eyes on Virginia. "Did she say when she'd be back?"

Virginia shook her head. *Should I tell him about Kim's weird behavior, how frightened she was? No. He'll just make a joke of it.*

"About your cartoon . . . ," Virginia said, changing the subject.

"Did you like it?" Trip wiggled his eyebrows. "I think I offended everybody this time."

"It was a quarter of an inch too wide."

"Arrrgh!" Trip clutched his throat. "Did you do emergency surgery with the matte knife?"

"Sorry." Virginia crossed from the light table to the computer next to Jo. "I gave the little guy in the corner the axe."

"Oh, man." Trip thrust his face up close to hers and demanded, "How could you? That guy is my signature. My trademark."

"I'm sorry, Trip, but you gave me no choice." Virginia nudged him aside and pushed a key on the computer board. The template for the second page appeared and she readjusted the margins. "You weren't here during the work session this morning. The deadline for your artwork was last week. The little muskrat, or penguin, or whatever it was you drew in the cartoon wasn't saying anything. He just stared out from the page like a piece of wood—"

Trip held up his hand like a traffic cop. "I get the point."

"Geez, Trip," Jo said from her workstation. "When are you going to let that dorky chipmunk speak? You put that thing in every cartoon, and he just sits there, like a rodent-shaped log."

"He's not a chipmunk, he's a weasel. All the great political cartoonists have little critters in the bottom corner of their cartoons, making comments on the comments. And he'll speak when—"

The door opened quietly and Emily Wolfe appeared, her long wool coat rustling against her dress. Trip pointed to her, a devilish twinkle in his eyes. "When Emily Wolfe laughs. Or when Pluto collides with Saturn. Whichever comes first."

Emily, a petite blonde with icy gray eyes, shot Trip a haughty look. "Draw something funny and maybe I'll laugh, Mr. McFadden." She tossed her books onto the tattered couch between the work stations and the door and settled in front of her computer. "I pasted up the editorial page copy yesterday, Virginia."

"I saw it, thanks." Virginia watched Emily rearrange the tiny vase of violets at her workstation, then tuck her curly blonde hair behind her ears. In her dark floral-print dress, Emily looked wonderfully feminine. "I kept the Star Gazer column on the left of this issue, Emily. But we might want to change the position for the next issue. You know, for interest."

"Horoscope columns should always be in the same place," Emily said softly. She lifted the dustcover from her keyboard with her delicate fingers. Her pale skin shone in its usual flawless way, making Virginia think of white roses. "That way people know where to look for them."

"Yeah, just like obituaries," Trip cracked.

"Do you think people really believe in astrology?" Virginia asked as she handed the horoscope column to Emily. "I mean, how can one statement apply to the millions of Virgos in the world?"

Emily took the paper. "They're just approximations based on the transits and conjunctions. I add my own touches, though, to smooth them out. You'd be amazed at how accurate a horoscope can be." She studied the piece of paper, then gave Virginia a dark look. "You changed something, I see." Her frown deepened.

"Just the spelling," Virginia said quickly.

"Sorry I'm late." Sam Calhoun, a tall, muscular African-American with a dazzling smile, stuck his head in the door. "My lab experiment self-destructed. I'll get that second page cleaned up."

Sam crossed to his workstation on Emily's right, flicked on the computer, and set to work rearranging text. Virginia was always impressed with the expert way Sam could deal with the mechanics of columns and margins. It was almost like he could see the rows of type in his head.

"Where's Kim?" Sam asked, tearing open a bag of Cheetos and stuffing a handful in his mouth. "She was helping me with this Science Club article."

Virginia turned back to the waxer and light table, measuring a row of ads for a local movie theater. "I don't know. I—"

"Arrrggghhhh!" Jo screamed from her computer station. Virginia jumped, and the hot waxer singed her finger. "Yeow!"

"What's wrong?" Trip and Sam cried at once.

"My computer!" Jo began punching keys at random. "It's not responding to any keystroke commands." Then, leaning forward, she began tugging at the tangle of cords at the back of the computer.

"Stop that, Jo!" Sam shouted. "You'll lose everything." He jumped up and, brushing aside the pile of dirty cups and crumpled paper on Jo's desk, tapped the keys.

"What's the matter with it?" Jo asked, running both hands through her spiked hair.

Sam worked a few more keys, then gave Virginia a discouraged look over his shoulder. "Crashed. That's funny. It's never crashed before. Jo, did you do something different?"

Jo shook her head.

"Could be a virus," Emily said, leaning back in her chair. "You should be more careful with all those disks you borrow, Jo. I run a virus checker every day."

It was Virginia's turn to scream. "Jo, you'll have to type in your copy on another computer. Hurry up! We're going to be late!"

Jo shrieked, then dove toward the big trash can parked beside the door. "I think I tossed a draft copy in here." She rooted in the bin frantically, flinging bunches of crumpled sheets of paper onto the floor. Virginia hurried over to help her.

"Do you see it?" Virginia asked.

"Not yet. I had such a wonderful quote from the team forward, too."

Emily snorted scornfully. "Isn't that a contradiction, Jo? Basketball players aren't known for their pithy insights."

"That's what I thought, too," Jo muttered, her head in the trash can. "But Matt does this visualization thing before he plays, and it sounds like he actually understands that whole 'inner game' idea. Oh, here it is!" She emerged from the trash can with a rumpled, stained piece of paper. "Yuck, Sam! Cut back on the cheese puffs, okay? That orange fallout sticks to everything."

"I didn't expect anyone to go through my trash," Sam grunted as he sat back down at his computer and hunched over the keys.

The door opened again, and Casey Collier hurried inside. Her well-groomed, shoulder-length auburn hair was windblown, her cheeks pink with cold.

Virginia looked up. "Dance photos. Tell me you have dance photos, Casey."

"Sorry," Casey said, wincing. "They didn't turn out. I took some shots of the new bike path for Jo's article instead."

Virginia felt the tightening knot of panic again, and clenched her jaw. "Why? Why does this stuff have to happen just before deadline? First Kim's late, and now you don't have the dance photos."

"Kim's not just late," Casey said, tossing her camera on her chair and getting a comb out of her tiny leather purse. "I overheard the secretary in the office say that Kim won't be back at all."

"What does that mean? Today? Or ever?"

"I don't know, but she sounded really worried." Casey ran the comb through her hair and tucked it back into her purse.

Virginia remembered Kim's frightened face, her glassy eyes. Something had really been troubling her earlier. But what? And was there a connection between the way Kim had been behaving and this new information about her not coming back?

"I think if Kim was going away she would have told me," Jo said, pausing in her typing. "But she has been pretty jumpy lately."

Emily shrugged. "Kim's a Gemini. They're changeable. One minute they're the life of the party—the next, withdrawn."

"Horoscopes," Virginia huffed. "I wonder if this is the 'unexpected surprise' mine mentioned. Personally, I always thought surprise meant something good. This is a disaster." She peeled off a waxed ad from the right-hand column and stuck it on the left. She rearranged the ad, then trimmed a smaller one to make it fit into the space left over.

"Horoscopes are totally bogus, Virginia," Trip said, handing her another ad. "You read one that says it'll be a great day, and you make yourself have a great day. You can't help yourself. It's . . . posthypnotic suggestion or something."

"I think you mean a self-fulfilling prophecy," Virginia said, tucking a strand of her long brown hair behind one ear.

"Not at all." Emily spun around to face them. Her hands were folded carefully in her lap. "Last August, my horoscope predicted that something truly magical was about to happen. And my boyfriend and I had a picnic in our secret garden—that's what I call the greenhouse in our backyard."

"So that's where you get those fresh flowers all winter long," Trip remarked, pointing at the small vase of violets on her desk. "I've wondered about that for months."

"Anyway, he picked a perfect rose and presented it to me." Emily smiled a sweet, misty smile. "That was magical."

Virginia swallowed over the lump in her throat. Even strange Emily had a boyfriend? Funny, she'd never mentioned one before.

"What sign are you, Emily?" Virginia asked.

"Pisces," Emily replied. "It's a water sign. Pisces is probably the most sensitive and intuitive sign in the Zodiac. Pisces are often psychic. We have vivid imaginations and can be very emotional."

And that gets you a boyfriend? Maybe Virgos are allergic to them. Virginia had certainly never had a steady boyfriend. Or a picnic in a garden greenhouse, where someone picked one perfect rose to give her.

"Yeah, but I read my horoscope all the time and it's never accurate," Jo said from Kim's computer as her fingers flew across the keys. "I mean, last week the newspaper said Scorpios were to make financial gains, and I got a speeding ticket that cost me fifty bucks."

Trip nodded his head. "My Leo horoscope this morning said I was going to meet a 'new friend' and 'communicate on a new level.'" He held out his hands in dismay. "So where are the babes?"

Emily held up one slim, tapered finger. "But it also said something about experiencing an 'odd misfortune.'"

Trip flopped in his chair. "Hey, that could be anything from a pop quiz in physics to my mom fixing liver for dinner."

Neat and orderly. That's what Virginia's horoscope had said about her. Virginia cocked her head and looked at her desk across the room. Every pencil was in its place, every paper filed perfectly away, and her bulletin board carefully arranged so that she could actually read everything on it. Her room at home was the same.

Bed made, desk neat, clothes hung all facing the same way and two inches apart in her closet. She even folded her clothes before she put them in the clothes hamper.

"But now and then those horoscopes really seem to hit the mark. Don't they?" Virginia asked the room in general.

Emily nodded. "You're a classic Virgo, Ginny. A practical, down-to-earth, compulsive worker. Virgos seem overly critical but it's just their way of analyzing the world. They can tend to worry too much."

"Me worry?" Virginia laughed, weakly. *All I do is worry.*

"That's true, you do worry," Casey said. "Remember when you lost that locket in September? Talk about compulsive. You were like Sherlock Holmes on the case."

"Virgos are born detectives," Emily interjected.

"I thought you were going to call in the FBI," Casey added.

"But it was my grandmother's locket. My most treasured possession." Virginia still hadn't gotten over losing her antique locket. She felt undressed without it. "I'm not compulsive. I just know what's important. And when something goes wrong I try to fix it."

"It's a good thing you don't lose stuff very often," Trip replied. "You were a basket case."

"I was not," Virginia huffed. "Now let's get back to work." She turned on one heel and marched around the room, collecting articles and reading them over. "At this rate, we'll be here till midnight."

Grumbling, they all returned to their computers. Trip and Virginia huddled around the light table. Emily waved the corrected Star Gazer column in the air, and Virginia added it to the pile of finished articles. Her eyes fell on the Virgo horoscope once more.

Neat and orderly. I've always been like this. Even in kindergarten, Virginia was the one who picked up the toys. *But there's nothing wrong with that. Especially in this job.* Being editor meant handling at least three crises a day. It was good to be well-organized.

They had worked in silence for nearly five minutes when Jo's raspy voice cut across the room. "Hey, Virginia. If Kim isn't coming back today, who's going to write the Heart-to-Heart column?"

"The column!" She hurried to Kim's desk and tried to open the drawer where Kim usually kept the Heart-to-Heart letters she was working on. "Where are the letters?" Virginia rifled through the papers stacked on top of the desk. "God, Jo, there are more of your assignments here than Kim's."

"Kim doesn't mind," Jo said with a shrug. Her stuff had a way of creeping across the desks. Actually, it had a way of creeping everywhere. "Check the bulletin board. Sometimes Kim pins letters there."

Virginia studied the wall of bulletin boards in front of the computers. Kim had pinned a series of pictures from fashion magazines of ultracool outfits, hairdos, and jewelry.

Virginia eyed them. "Don't you think it's strange the way Kim hangs up a picture of an outfit one week, and the next she's wearing practically the exact same thing? It's like she waves a magic wand and they materialize out of nowhere."

Jo ran her hand through her now drooping spikes. "I don't know how she does it, but she's got a great eye. Like a fashion designer. And she always looks totally cool."

Virginia thought about the way Kim had looked that morning. Rumpled, in an old red sweater and torn jeans. *Almost uncool.* She gave Kim's desk one more quick search. "No Heart-to-Heart letters. Anywhere."

"I bet the incoming letters are in her file," Sam said, rising from his keyboard and heaving an empty pretzel bag in the trash can. "Kim is very organized about the column."

Virginia joined him at the filing cabinets just as he pulled out a bulging folder. "Yep, here they are." Sam flicked it open and pulled out the first letter. "Hey, listen, you guys. 'My boyfriend keeps flirting with other girls. He watches them walk past us in the halls. Should I dump him?'" Sam looked up at Virginia, a twinkle in his eyes. "Should she?"

"How should I know?" Virginia cried. "I'm not exactly an expert on relationships. I can't answer this stuff."

"You're the editor," Trip called from the light table, where he was still rearranging page two. "You're in charge. You've gotta do it."

Virginia folded her arms across her chest and scowled at Trip, who seemed to be enjoying her discomfort.

He stared back affably. "Who else is going to do it? You're logical, sensible."

"You always get top grades," Sam added. "The teachers think you're the greatest thing since canned tuna."

"You even take the grocery carts back to the store from the parking lot." Trip slapped his fist into his palm. "Those lonelyhearts out there need a good dose of Virginia Wells and her common sense."

"Oh, all right," Virginia muttered, grabbing the file from Sam. She knew they were just teasing but the barbs hurt anyway. They made her sound like some kind of Goody Two-shoes.

Virginia sank down on the couch in their makeshift lounge. There was a hot plate next to it where she heated her tea each day. And an old sink covered in crusted globs of different-colored paint. Big metal shelf units stacked with supplies that they never used lined the walls on either side of the couch. It wasn't exactly attractive, but it was their own special retreat.

Glancing through the top few letters, Virginia saw they were pretty ordinary. "'Why do boys have to be the ones who always ask girls out?'" she read out loud. "Because," she answered.

Everyone laughed. "You're going to have to do better than that," Trip called.

Virginia flipped to the next letter. "'Cheerleading tryouts are unfair.'" The staff made disgusted noises. "Life's unfair," Virginia replied.

"'All the boys I like never notice me. Never notice I'm alive . . .'"

Virginia put it on the maybe pile. It sounded like one she could answer. Too easily. After all, she'd had plenty of crushes over the years on the wrong boys. And she'd recovered—eventually. *I might even be able to offer some good advice.*

She skimmed a few more. All pretty ordinary. "'The popular crowd runs this school.'" So, what else was new?

She flipped to the letter at the very bottom of the stack. And stopped short.

If you cut me, I will bleed. If you hurt me—I will die. He hurt me. My heart aches. I am dying. I want him to know my pain.

Desperate

Virginia inhaled sharply. This letter was different. *Scary.*

The last-period bell jangled above her head, and she jumped at the sound. One hour to go. Virginia decided to pick just a few of the other letters and compose some quick replies for the column. She'd worry about answering the rest later.

"Come on, guys," she said, leaping to her feet. "We have exactly one hour! I'll have to use the computer in Ms. Burns's office to do these letters. Have the paste-up finished by the time I get back."

"Yes, boss," Trip and Jo hollered, their voices following her out the door. As she hurried across the quad toward the main building, she thought about that last letter sent to the Heart-to-Heart column.

He hurt me. . . . I am dying. I want him to know my pain.

Whoever wrote that was either seriously disturbed or some sort of sick practical joker. Either way, it gave her the creeps.

c h a p t e r 3

There he is. The winner of the Virginia Wells Longest-standing Crush Award.

Virginia had just pulled the garage door shut and was in the process of carrying two of her mother's grocery bags into the house when she saw the porch light flick on next door.

Jake Morris stepped out of his front door and stood for a moment in the golden light. He was smiling.

Virginia froze, half-hoping he'd notice her and half-hoping he wouldn't. Dressed in baggy tweeds, a turtleneck, and a fisherman's sweater, Jake looked drop-dead gorgeous. As usual.

He'd been the secret love of Virginia's life for

years. Tall, broad-shouldered, with sandy blond hair and green eyes, he was definitely the "white knight" type. And when they were children, he had always come to her rescue, helping her down out of trees when she lost her nerve and bringing her Band-Aids when she skinned her knees. One Halloween, when some bullies stole her bag of candy, he gallantly gave her his own.

When he got older Jake would mow their lawn in the summers with his shirt off. Virginia would hang out her bedroom window, drooling.

He used to be her buddy. And now? Jake thought of her—if he thought of her at all—as his sister's baby-sitter. *How boring.*

Virginia gave him one more longing look, and sighed. She shifted the grocery bags higher in her arms and stepped onto her front porch.

"Hey, Ginny! Wait up!"

Virginia spun, nearly dropping the bag with the soup cans and a jar of mayonnaise. *I don't believe it. He's coming over.* Virginia just had time to yank her hair out from under her jacket and stick the grocery bag with the toilet paper inside the front door, before he was standing in front of her on her porch steps. "Oh. Hi, Jake."

"How ya doing?" he asked.

"Good. I'm doing fine." She grinned like a dope. "We made our deadline at the paper, though the articles were too short and the ads too big. We even had to fill in some extra space with a calendar of events from our files. Not exactly an award-winning edition, but it's finished."

Will you shut up? "How are you doing?" does not mean, "Tell me your life's story."

Jake didn't seem to notice that Virginia was blathering like an idiot. He shoved his hands in his pockets and cocked his head, so that a lock of his hair fell across his forehead. "You going to the game? Big grudge match, you know, with Anderson High. Man, am I psyched."

Virginia frantically tried to recall the sports article about the upcoming game. "Yeah, Matt will have his hands full with that Anderson power forward." She held her breath. Maybe Jake wouldn't notice she was quoting directly from Jo's article.

Jake gave her a surprised look. "That's right. Rob Collins. He scored twenty points against Ferndale last week."

"I know." Virginia shifted her remaining bag of groceries onto her hip. "Great baseline move. Good fallaway jump shot, too."

"Whoa, you know your basketball." Jake nodded appreciatively. "Are you going tonight?"

Are you kidding? I never go to the games. I'd be all by myself, is what Virginia wanted to stay. Instead, she shook her head. "I don't think so."

Jake put one foot on her porch railing and leaned forward. "You gotta go. I mean, the team's counting on us to give our support." He reached out and flicked the tip of her nose. He had been doing that for ten years. "We can't let the school down. We really have to be there."

We? Was Jake asking her to go with him? "I—I guess you're right," Virginia stammered.

He grinned, revealing the dimple in his right cheek. "You bet I am. Come on, you can ride with me. My car's running."

Virginia's face flushed pink with pleasure. *Is this a dream come true, or what?* "I need to take the groceries inside and get my purse. If you can wait a minute . . ."

"Sure. We don't mind. But make it snappy. Tiff wants to get a good seat."

"Tiff?" Virginia felt the sizzling joy go poof.

"Yeah. Tiffany Summers. You know her, don't you?"

Virginia looked toward Jake's car. Vaguely,

through the frosty windows, she could detect the outline of another person. *He already has a date.*

Of course Jake wasn't asking her out. He was just being friendly. Inviting her to tag along with his girlfriend, like a kid sister. *Do I feel stupid, or what?*

"I'll go tell Tiff you're on your way." Jake turned to jog toward his car.

"No, don't!" Virginia shouted louder than she'd intended. It stopped Jake in his tracks. He spun to look at her, and she said quickly, "I just remembered, I promised Mom I would help her put away the groceries and, um, make cookies this evening."

Make cookies? What a geeky thing to say.

"Well, if you're sure . . ." Jake backed slowly across the lawn.

"I'm sorry, it's just that I promised Mom and, you know . . ." Pasting a broad smile on her face, Virginia forced her voice to sound cheerful. "You and Tiffany have a terrific time, and be sure to let me know who hits a homer."

"That's baseball," he said, a quizzical look on his face.

"I knew that." Virginia fumbled to get the front screen door open. "I was just joking." *Get me out of here.*

Jake waved, then hurried to his car and hopped in. As he drove away, Virginia yanked the screen door open and one of the paper grocery bags ripped apart at the seams. All of its contents, including a full carton of eggs, tumbled out onto her front porch.

"Oh, great. Just great," she said, trying to scoop up the dripping mess with the carton lid. "The perfect end to a lousy day."

When she finally managed to get everything back into the bags and the front door open, Virginia marched through the living room into the kitchen, plunked the bags on the counter, then raced straight to her room. She could still feel her face burning from the humiliation of assuming Jake had asked her for a date.

"Dinner in fifteen minutes," her mom's voice called from the kitchen.

"I'm not hungry," Virginia muttered, pulling off her wool coat and throwing herself on her bed. "I'm depressed."

Virginia's purse and books lay on her desk, and the Heart-to-Heart letters had fallen out of their file onto the floor by her bed. From where she lay she could just read the last words on one of the letters.

My heart aches. I am dying. I want him to know my pain.

"Tell me about it," Virginia murmured as she reached for the typewritten page.

That afternoon, Virginia had written answers to three of the Heart-to-Heart letters. She knew she hadn't managed Kim's sincere and understanding touch, but she'd been practical and sensible. Which would have to do.

She stared down at this letter, a definite cry for help, and felt real empathy for the writer. "My heart aches, too."

Because of space limitations, Kim answered only three or four letters each month in the *Spectator*. But during the weeks between issues, she made a point of responding to all the others. She always dropped those replies in a heart-shaped wooden mailbox nailed to the outside of the Bungalow.

Virginia decided she would do that, too. *After all, I've known disappointment in love. I've felt my confidence being chipped away, little by little.*

Virginia got up from her bed and opened her desk drawer. Inside were several sheets of neatly laid out, cream-colored stationery with her initials, VLW (L for Laine), embossed in gold at the top. She kept her special fountain pens in a carved wooden box on the first shelf above the desk. *Neat and orderly. That's me.*

She sat at the small oak desk, her pen poised above the blank sheet of paper. How many guys had she really liked? A lot. And not one of them had ever looked at her as if she were anything special. Oh, she had dated. Still did, now and then. Occasionally, she went out with the same guy twice. But never more than that. Things just never worked out.

Virginia bent her head and began to write.

Dear Desperate,

    I want you to know you're not alone. My heart aches, too. The boys I like don't like me. I don't know why that is but I'm learning to accept it. Part of it is, I've always lacked the courage to tell them how I feel. Maybe you should try that. Talk to this boy. Tell him you're hurting. Maybe he doesn't know. Whatever he says, just remember—you are a good person.

Heart

Virginia crossed the *t* in "Heart," then carefully folded the letter and tucked it into an envelope.

I don't know if this will help her, but at least she'll know she's not alone.

She tucked the letter in her purse, planning to drop it in the Outgoing box on Monday.

Brrring!

The ringing of the phone downstairs broke the silence and Virginia nearly jumped out of her skin. "Boy, it has been a bad day," she muttered, picking up the pen she'd dropped.

"Virginia! It's for you," her mom called up the stairs.

She hurried down into the kitchen, ignoring the fact that her mother was waving her hand toward the dinner table.

"Hello?"

"Hey, Virginia. Trip here. I—I'm at school. Why aren't you here?"

Virginia grinned into the phone. "Because I'm here."

Trip didn't chuckle. "I think you should be here. I'm at the game. You know, the basketball game?"

"There's a basketball game?" Virginia gasped in mock surprise. "You're kidding. Only half of the entire paper was devoted to interviews with the team, and the schedule has been plastered all over the school walls for weeks, and—"

"Yeah, yeah, I know," Trip cut in, impatiently.

The public phone in the gym was near the basketball court, and Virginia could hear the crowd screaming and the squeaks of sneakered feet on the wooden floor. Trip raised his voice to shout over the noise. "What I meant to say is, could you come down here? Something's wrong."

Virginia felt that tension knot in her stomach, which had just begun to loosen from the day's pressure, press into her middle. "Nothing's happened to the paper, has it?" What if the printer had lost the whole edition, and they had to start all over?

"No, no. But . . . well, I've heard some really . . . strange news."

Virginia wrinkled her forehead. Trip sounded odd. Like he was nervous. Or scared. "What news?"

A burst of cheering erupted from the gym and Trip had to wait for it to subside before he could answer.

"It's about Kim. She's disappeared."

"What?" Virginia felt her throat tighten with fear. "What do you mean? Kim ran away?"

"That's what people are saying. Her parents are totally freaked out."

A wave of guilt instantly washed over Virginia. *I should have said something to someone this morning when she acted so scared.*

Her mother tapped her on the shoulder from behind and pointed again at the waiting dinner. Her dad frowned at her from his place at the table.

Virginia scowled back at him and mouthed, "I'll be there in a minute. This is important."

A buzzer sounded and the rumbling of the crowd got louder.

"There's more," Trip shouted. "I went out behind the gym to toss my sweatshirt in my car, it's like a sauna in here, and I noticed the lights on in the newsroom."

"I'm sure I turned them off when I left," Virginia said.

"I thought you did, too, so I went over to check it out—and I found something weird."

Why was Trip being so mysterious? This was a guy who always said exactly what was on his mind. "Spit it out, Trip. What did you find?"

"Sorry, Virginia, but it's just so—bizarre. I think you have to see it for yourself."

Virginia wrinkled her forehead. She wondered if this was just Trip's warped sense of humor at work again. As well as she knew him, it was hard to tell.

She'd had a crush on Trip when she was a sophomore. They'd met in the Creative Writing Club at school. His wackiness appealed to her, and his artistic talent had always amazed her. Trip could draw anything. He'd even done a portrait of her, sort of as a joke, and it was really good. She still had it tucked away in her desk.

Fortunately, she'd gotten over him before she'd been appointed editor. Working with him and suffering the pangs of unrequited love at the same time would have been the pits.

"Is this a joke?" she asked. "Are you going to get me down there so that you can dump water on my head or something?"

"No! I wouldn't kid around about this, Virginia. Especially not with you. Just come over, okay?"

He really sounded jittery. Not like Trip at all.

"Okay, okay. I'll be right there."

Virginia hung up the phone and raced for the stairs. "I've got to go to school for a little bit. Trip needs help on—on a piece he's doing for the paper."

"Not without dinner, young lady," her dad

said. He gave her his do-it-and-don't-ask-any-questions look.

"All right." Virginia moved obediently to the dinner table. *I'm seventeen, the editor of the high school newspaper, and they treat me like a kid. Humiliating.*

Virginia ate as fast as possible, wolfing down her spaghetti and salad. Then she bolted from the table, grabbed her coat and purse, and raced out the door.

Luckily, Fairview High was only three blocks from her house. The night was cold, and Virginia huddled into her down jacket as she dodged the bare bushes bordering the sidewalk. Shadows engulfed her, and the wind rustled the bare limbs above her head.

Things don't feel right. Walk faster. Virginia quickened her pace. Soon the lights surrounding the school dispelled the murky darkness.

The front parking lot was full. Kids moved in and out of the shadows, some arriving at the game, some leaving. Lights blazed from the gym, and the screams of fans poured from the open doors. She thought about Jake Morris and his date, and all the other kids and their friends, cheering and having a good time.

Virginia crossed behind a row of cars, and stopped as she recognized a figure standing next to a dark blue pickup. It was Casey Collier, talking to three boys.

"Casey? What are you doing out here? You're supposed to be inside taking pictures."

Casey was snuggled into the heavy jacket of one of the boys, and she didn't look pleased to see Virginia. "Oh. Hi, Ginny. Yeah, I'm on my way."

"Then get a move on." Virginia knew she sounded like a den mother, but the newspaper always needed good sports-action shots. Casey usually came up short.

Casey stuck out her lower lip. "Virginia, you can be such a drag. I was just getting some more film from my car."

Yeah, sure. Casey's red sports car was on the other side of the parking lot. "Where's your camera?"

"In the gym." Casey put her hands on her hips. "I didn't want the lens to frost up. Is that okay?"

Casey's smart remark surprised Virginia. "Of course it's okay. Do whatever you want."

"I will." Casey gestured for the boys to follow her back to the gym, which was at the other end of the school building. "Come on, you guys."

"Don't leave me with the ice queen," a boy in

glasses called, jogging after them. "My lenses are starting to frost up."

They all laughed and hurried away.

Ice queen? Is that what they think of me? Virginia was mystified. She could feel not just her face but the tips of her ears burning with embarrassment.

"Jerks," she grumbled. Virginia flipped up her collar and walked quickly along the building, skirting the parking lot. As she rounded the end of the school, she caught a glimpse of someone across the lot. The figure, shrouded in shadow, paused, looked toward her, then ducked behind some cars. Faint footsteps echoed in the distance. Then silence.

Who was that? Obviously not Casey. Virginia frowned. Whoever it was hadn't wanted to be seen. *Odd.*

She crossed the grass toward the Bungalow. Lifting the hinged lid of the heart-shaped Outgoing Heart-to-Heart box, she dropped her note to Desperate inside.

"Virginia, is that you?" Trip called.

"Yes." Virginia pulled open the Bungalow door, then paused and looked back over her shoulder. Was someone watching her? She couldn't see anyone.

"I'm over here." Trip stood at the light table, the glow of the lamp casting an eerie white sheen on his face.

"What is it, Trip?"

Trip pointed to the door. "Look behind you. There."

Virginia turned and gasped. A matte knife was stuck in the door, its handle jutting out at a grotesque angle.

"I found it when I came into the room," Trip explained. "And look. Over here."

Virginia joined him at the light table. Pieces of a photograph lay scattered across the surface. It appeared to have been a picture of the basketball team. Virginia recognized some of the faces among the slashed pieces.

"It's been hacked into little tiny bits," he said.

Virginia turned to look at the door. "With that knife?" she asked.

"I think so," he said. "I thought you should see this because . . . I don't know, there's just something creepy about it."

"Maybe it's a prank," she suggested. "You know, like when kids spray-paint the halls, or break windows."

"Maybe," Trip agreed. "But if they had really

wanted to trash the newsroom, they would've overturned files and thrown paper everywhere, or spilled ink on something. This . . ." He gestured toward the light table. "This seems so methodical."

Virginia looked at the remnants of the photo. Bits of faces and eyes stared at her. "What's that?" she asked. Dark little dots were sprinkled over the photo and table like a fine mist.

"What?"

"Those little specks. They cover the table."

Trip reached out and touched one of the dots on a corner of photograph. He pulled his fingertip away. It was smeared with red.

Trip raised his head and whispered, "It's blood, Virginia. Blood."

c h a p t e r 4

The Moon and Uranus have combined in a strange aspect, sowing confusion about your friends and their motives. You'll have to go deep beneath the surface to figure this one out. With your obsession for detail and sharp analytical mind, you're a born detective. Start digging, Virgo.

Early Monday morning an exhausted Virginia stood with Trip on the sidewalk in front of the school. Sam and Jo Plunkett had joined her and Trip at the copy shop on Saturday and the four of them had run off over a thousand flyers. It had been an all-school effort to post the flyers on every telephone pole, in every store window, and on every bulletin board in town.

"This is my last flyer," Virginia said, carefully sticking the four pushpins into the corners, making sure they held firmly. She read the poster one more time.

MISSING: KIM KELLER

Age: 17   Ht: 5' 4"   Wt: 110 lbs.

Eyes: BROWN   Hair: BROWN

Last seen Friday morning at Fairview High School.
If you have any information regarding her whereabouts,
please contact the Fairview police.

Trip studied the grainy class picture skepti-
cally. "Do you really think that photo looks like
Kim?"

Virginia shrugged. "It was the best we could
do on short notice. Somehow all of Kim's pictures have disappeared from the files. It's a good
thing Emily thought of last year's annual."

A strong gust of wind threatened to tear the
flyer off the telephone pole, but it held fast.
Virginia shivered and Trip took her by the
elbow. "It feels like snow. Come on. I think we
better get inside."

They crossed the nearly deserted parking lot
and headed toward the Bungalow, huddling
together against the fierce wind.

"I hope those flyers help," Virginia murmured, trying to keep her teeth from chattering.

"The police have sent a description of Kim

and her car to every county in Kansas, and even into the bordering states," Trip answered. "And her mom and dad are calling relatives and friends to see if she's contacted any of them. Something should turn up soon."

Virginia nodded. "It's not like Kim to just go off completely on her own. At least I don't think she'd do something that foolish."

"Yeah, she's usually pretty level-headed," Trip replied.

Virginia squeezed her eyes shut. They burned from lack of sleep. All weekend the image of Kim's frightened face had kept appearing in her mind. And her anguished voice, crying out, "I can't take any more."

Virginia hadn't spent much time thinking about the weird incident with the matte knife and the photograph. But whenever she tried to fall asleep, the light table and the blood-spattered pieces of photograph would materialize in her head.

Should she have reported it to Ms. Burns? Probably. For some reason, she'd felt an instinctive reluctance to tell the adviser. At least she didn't want to yet.

"So many odd things have happened in the

last few days," Virginia said to Trip. "It feels like our normally sane world has tilted."

Trip nodded. "I don't know if the knife and blood had anything to do with Kim's disappearance, but it's weird that everything went so haywire at once."

Virginia thought about the Heart-to-Heart letters. "Maybe it's the planets lining up in some strange configuration," she said.

"That's something Emily would know about," Trip said with a chuckle. "She's the queen of horoscopes."

"Say." Virginia stopped and stared at Trip. "Didn't yours warn about an odd misfortune? Maybe that meant the strange stuff you found in the Bungalow."

"Yeah, but that didn't happen directly to me," Trip reminded her, "so it wasn't my misfortune."

"Let's hope nothing does happen to you," Virginia said, suppressing a shiver.

Trip rolled his eyes. "I told you that astrology stuff is bunk. Totally bogus bunk."

By this time they'd reached the lawn that stretched between the Bungalow and the rest of the school. Trip turned toward the main building. "I have to talk to Mr. Cooney. We agreed to have a serious discussion about my calculus work. It should be short and to the point." Trip knit his brows together in imitation of the math teacher. "Give it up, McFadden."

Virginia would have laughed but her teeth were chattering too loudly. "Yeah."

"I'll catch you later," Trip said, cupping his hands over his ears to keep them warm. "Call me if you hear any word about Kim."

"And you do the same," Virginia replied. Then she turned and sprinted for the Bungalow. Flinging open the door, Virginia hopped inside. The air was nearly as icy as outside. But that wasn't what caused Virginia to freeze.

Something's different. Changed. But what?

Virginia quickly spun to look at the back of the door, then sighed in relief when she saw nothing there. Trip had gathered up the pieces of the picture and the knife and put them away. "No use freaking out the staff," he had said Friday night.

What's different?

Virginia closed her eyes, picturing clearly the room as she remembered it from Friday. Casey's boxes of stock photos lining the outer wall. The four computers. Jo's empty soda cans and candy bar wrappers. Kim's pictures. Emily's flowers.

More of Jo's junk. Sam's computer disks. The light table. Trip's art supplies. The polished wooden floor. Her own neat desk along the right-hand wall. The kitchen in the back.

She shook her head and opened her eyes. *Maybe if I go out and come in again, I'll be able to tell what it is.* Stepping outside, Virginia took a deep breath of cold air. On impulse, she flicked up the lid to the Outgoing box. Her letter to Desperate was gone. She lifted the lid to the Incoming box. A letter lay propped against the side of the box. This one was written on lavender paper. She read it quickly.

> *Dear Heart,*
>
> *I guess I'm not good enough for him. He ignores me now. I thought he kind of liked me. But I was wrong. What's the matter with me?*
>
> *Nobody*

Not from Desperate this time. From another lost soul. She glanced around quickly, surveying the empty quad. Another gust of wind slammed the lid shut on the wooden box. The wind felt as if it were blowing in from Alaska across Nebraska, and straight into her corner of Kansas.

Virginia stepped back inside and looked at the workstations again. She studied each one: Sam's, Emily's, Kim's . . . Jo's. That was it. Jo's desk was cleaned up. *Now when did she do that?* When they'd all left Friday, it was covered with paper, candy wrappers, empty soda cans, and two plastic water bottles. Now the desktop was completely bare. Not a bubble gum wrapper in sight. And Emily's flowers were different, too. A bouquet of tiny pink roses sat in the blue vase.

That's funny. There were violets Friday.

Still clutching the letter from Nobody, Virginia flicked on the hot plate, filled a kettle with water, then moved to her desk. She opened the file of Heart-to-Heart letters. On top was the letter from Desperate, word-processed on standard computer paper. Ordinary. Generic. She set the lavender note from Nobody on top. Desperate must have picked up her response letter sometime between Friday night and Monday morning. And Nobody's note must have come over the weekend, too. *Strange.*

She pulled out a piece of paper from her desk. *Might as well answer Nobody now, before school starts.*

"Dear Nobody," she wrote. "Nothing is

wrong with you. Sometimes things don't work out, that's all. Be kind to yourself and think of one thing you can do today that will make you feel special. Maybe volunteer to help someone else. You are a valuable person."

After signing the note, "Heart," Virginia went back outside, dropped it in the Outgoing box, then turned and nearly collided with Casey.

"Yikes!" Virginia screamed.

"Sorry, Ginny. Didn't mean to scare you."

It was the first she'd seen Casey since their embarrassing exchange on Friday night. "That's all right," Virginia said, feeling a bit awkward. "I didn't expect to see anyone this early." She opened the door for Casey and followed her into the Bungalow, not wanting to look her in the eye.

"What are you doing here?" Casey asked, removing her coat. As usual, she looked like a model for a preppy fashion magazine: pressed chino slacks, a pale pink sweater adorned with a fine gold chain, and penny loafers. Her shoulder-length hair was neatly arranged in a headband. "I mean, we got the paper out, didn't we?"

"I was putting up flyers for Kim, and I thought I'd answer some of the Heart-to-Heart letters." Virginia moved to her desk and pushed the letters back into their folder. "Why are *you* here?"

"I have a photo shoot this morning. The National Merit scholars." Casey crossed to the filing cabinets and pulled open the second drawer where the file photos were kept. "You haven't seen my extra film, have you?"

Virginia frowned. "If you're looking for film, why are you searching in the drawer marked File Photos?"

"This is where I keep it. But it's not here." Casey rummaged in the next drawer, then threw up her hands. "Why does stuff keep disappearing around here? It's so frustrating." She crossed to the windows that ran along the east wall. On the wide sill were several shoe boxes labeled Copies, Negatives, and Stock. Casey opened the Negatives box and pulled out a roll of film. Virginia stared at her. "Have you always kept film in the Negatives box?"

"Yep." Casey unwrapped the film and began loading her camera. "I've discovered if I'm very clever about my hiding places, people won't steal my supplies."

"Steal?" Virginia was flabbergasted. "That's the first I've heard of it."

"Oh, yes. My film has been walking off all year. And pens. I've never lost any money but I always make sure not to bring my wallet out here."

"I can't believe it. A thief in our building?" Virginia thought of the matte knife and the cutup photo on Friday night. She crossed to Casey's side. "I know this may sound like an odd question, but you didn't by any chance slice up a picture of the basketball team, did you?"

"Are you kidding? Cut up my own work?" Casey snapped her camera cover closed. "Trip told me about that. The only thing I can figure out is someone on the team didn't like the way their picture turned out. The guys are always complaining that my shots aren't very flattering." She snorted derisively. "As if they were photogenic or something. It's all I can do to make sure they don't look like gorillas."

"But it was sort of strange the way that picture was cut up," Virginia prodded. "Don't you think?"

Casey raised the camera to one eye and fiddled with the focus. "What d'ya mean?"

"The way the picture was sliced. Like a . . . a mutilation."

Casey lowered her camera. "Oh, come on, Virginia. You're exaggerating."

"I don't think so." Virginia dropped her voice in case someone was standing outside the door. "Is anyone angry at you? I mean—could someone have sliced that picture to get back at you?"

"Me? Are you crazy? No one in his, or her, right mind would— " She stopped, and a silly grin spread across her face. "Wait a second. Brooke's ticked off because Matthew Harrison wants to go out with me. She's been drooling over him for weeks." Casey rolled her eyes. "As if Matthew would look twice at Brooke."

"But it doesn't make sense for Brooke to cut up a picture of the guys on the basketball team," Virginia replied.

"You're right," Casey said with a chuckle. "She's in love with most of them. Or so she keeps telling everyone."

"What about the guys on the team itself?" Virginia asked. "Are any of them feuding?"

Casey squinted one eye shut. "Let's see. There's Matthew. He wants to go out with me. And Cody Jenkins. He does, too. We go to the same country club. Then there's Adam Fellows, the new guy. A total unknown. And Skip Parker, who's either studying for chemistry tests or shooting free throws. Troy Lennon is a total geek, so who cares what he thinks. And Joe Hayden has Brillo for brains." Casey shrugged. "I don't know. A few of the guys don't really hang with the group. But they all seem to get along fine."

Virginia had pulled a piece of paper out of her desk and was making notes as she asked questions. It helped her to think better. "Maybe someone who didn't make the team cut up the picture."

"Maybe. But it's a stupid way to get revenge." Casey slipped on her jacket. "I wouldn't waste much time worrying about it, Virginia."

A tall, dark-haired guy poked his head into the room. "Come on, Casey. We're freezing our you-know-whats off out here."

"Sorry, Chad. Be right there." Casey looped the camera strap over her shoulder, smiled at Virginia, then headed toward the door.

Virginia moved to the hot plate, where her water was boiling. *Why* would *someone cut up a photograph?* She filled her cup with hot water and dipped her tea bag into it. As she dunked the bag, Virginia suddenly felt a tingling sensation on the back of her neck. As if someone were behind her watching.

"Mr. Stevens wants to see the entire staff in the office pronto," Emily said from the door in a quiet voice.

Virginia jumped, spilling her tea.

"Good heavens, Emily. You scared me. I didn't hear you come in."

Trip pushed into the room behind Emily. "We're wanted in the office. Geez, school hasn't even started, and we're already in trouble."

"We're not in trouble," Emily said, carefully removing the small pink roses from their vase on her desk and replacing them with fresh ones. She tossed the old ones, which looked perfectly fine to Virginia, in the trash. "They just want to speak to us."

Casey, who had stopped at the door when Emily came in, complained, "This means I'll have to reschedule the Merit scholars. And it took me two weeks to get them together for this shot!"

Trip crossed to the file cabinets. "I was waylaid by the vice principal on my way to see Mr. Cooney. For some weird reason, they want to see all the back issues of the *Spectator*. Plus every Heart-to-Heart letter Kim received."

"I'll get the Heart-to-Heart letters," Virginia said, joining him at the file cabinet.

"Do you think they've heard something? About Kim?"

Trip shrugged. "I hope so."

Virginia yanked out the file with the Heart-to-Heart letters in it. The letter from Desperate was right on top. What would the principal say when he saw that? Probably cancel the column. Which would be a disaster. Virginia quickly slid the letter out of the file and stuck it under her pile of textbooks on her way to the door.

Virginia, Trip, Emily, and Casey hurried across the icy quad into the main building.

"I'll meet you at the office as soon as I cancel the photo shoot," Casey cried, running off down the hall toward the cafeteria.

As the group passed the lab, Sam Calhoun rushed out, his white lab coat flapping. His face was rigid with irritation.

"What's this all about? I was right in the middle of an experiment in chem lab. Adam Fellows and I were trying to finish our science project before school."

"We think it's about Kim," Virginia answered.

Sam stopped. "Oh. You sure?"

"It might be about that cartoon, Trip," Emily suggested as they headed toward the main hall.

"Do you think so?" Virginia gasped. "I mean, it was a little vicious, but all of Trip's cartoons are that way."

Trip sent Emily an angry glance. "It's probably about Virginia's editorial."

Virginia winced. "You might be right." She had been criticizing the Student Council lately. Before she could ask Trip what he thought was wrong with her article, they rounded a corner and practically fell over Jo Plunkett.

She was kneeling in front of her locker, yanking out piles of debris. Her spiky hair was even more disordered than ever, her face flushed.

"What are you doing, Jo?" Virginia asked.

Trip pointed to Jo's T-shirt, which was stained with what appeared to be the remains of a taco. "You look like you've been to a food fight in a phone booth."

Jo gave him an irritated look. "I've been asked—no—*ordered* to bring everything in this locker that belonged to Kim to the office." She drew her hand through her hair and shook her head. "I don't even remember whose junk is whose."

There was a thick Band-Aid on her right index finger.

"What happened to your hand?" Sam asked.

"Oh, my stupid cat thought it was breakfast. Her favorite trick these days is sharpening her fangs on my skin."

Jo pawed through the mound of stuff on the floor. Candy wrappers, notebooks, magazines, and books lay in one pile. There were pencils, erasers covered with brown fuzz, cola cans, two baseball caps, and some clothes in the other.

Trip studied the debris. "Jo, you're going to need a U-Haul."

"Kim's not going to like this," Jo muttered, scooping up the clothes and the baseball caps. "She's very private about her things. She won't appreciate it when she finds out her stuff is in the office."

Her arms full, Jo fell in step beside Emily. Casey hurried to join them.

"Boy, those Merit scholars were upset. They'd practically gotten frostbite waiting for me, then I had to cancel. If they weren't so determined to have their pictures in the paper, I'd say forget the whole thing."

The group hurried down the last hall to the office, and Virginia pushed open the door.

"Come in," Ms. Wilcox, the vice principal, said, ushering them toward the wide inner doors leading to the principal's office. She gestured toward a ring of chairs facing the principal's wooden desk. "Sit there."

Mr. Stevens sat behind the huge oak desk, looking very stern. Next to him on his right was their adviser, Ms. Burns.

Her face was ashen, and she looked away when Virginia tried to catch her eye. That wasn't like her. It almost looked as if she'd been crying.

On the principal's left sat a short chubby woman with dark hair and red cheeks. Virginia didn't recognize her.

Something's very, very wrong.

"I'll get right to the point," Mr. Stevens declared, focusing his eyes on Virginia. "Do you have any idea why Kim Keller would have been upset on Friday?"

"No, not really." Virginia didn't want to mention their argument. It certainly wasn't reason enough for Kim to run away. "She's been awfully moody lately."

"Yeah, usually Kim gets her assignments in on time," Trip added. "But the last few weeks she's been a little lax."

Sam Calhoun nodded. "She used to do a lot of her work in the Bungalow with the rest of us, but lately she's picked up the Heart-to-Heart letters and taken them home to answer."

The woman beside Mr. Stevens gestured at the file Virginia was carrying. "Are those the letters?" she asked, holding out her hand.

Virginia nodded and handed the file to her.

"This is Ms. Denson. She's a counselor," Mr. Stevens explained. "Now we know Kim's a good student. Well-behaved, liked by everyone. But is there anything unusual about her? Something teachers wouldn't notice?"

"Kim is a total clotheshorse," Casey answered, trying to smile. "You know, a new outfit every day, practically. I wish my parents would buy me new clothes like that. Jewelry, too."

Jo was looking down at the carpet.

"Would you agree with that, Jo?" Mr. Stevens asked.

Jo nodded, and Virginia could see she was worried. "Yeah. That's why our locker is so . . ."

"Terminal," Trip muttered.

"Shut up," Emily snapped.

"Kim always changes her clothes when she gets to school," Jo said. "The new outfits are always flashy, you know. With lots of extras. I guess her parents think they're too wild. The outfits, I mean. That's why she doesn't wear them at home."

Trip crossed his arms in front of him. "Do you have a reason for questioning us? I mean, I don't want to be a pain—"

Emily jabbed a finger into his ribs. "Then be quiet."

Trip brushed her hand away.

Mr. Stevens sighed and shook his head. "I know this is a little irregular. But since you work with Kim on a daily basis, we thought we could get a clearer picture of her from you students. Jo, do you spend much free time with Kimberly?"

"Yes, but I've never been to her house or anything. Now and then we go to a movie or for pizza in her old beater."

Trip gave Jo a surprised look. "Oh, that's right. I forgot she has that ancient car. I hardly ever see her drive it to school. It's green, right?"

Jo nodded. "She's embarrassed by it. But it runs. Barely."

"I sympathize," Trip said. "My bumper's tied on with a rope."

Ms. Burns cleared her throat. "Have any of

you noticed anything else out of the ordinary about Kim?"

Casey smoothed her hands over her slacks. "She asked me for all the pictures of her in the photo file a couple of weeks ago. I gave them to her, and she didn't return them."

"Do you know why she wanted them?" Ms. Burns asked, her round face worried.

Casey shook her head.

"Did she have boyfriend problems?" Ms. Denson asked.

"She doesn't have one," Emily replied.

"And even if she did, she wouldn't talk about it," Jo added. "Kim is a really private person. I mean, once she went to the movies with Greg Smith and didn't tell me. I heard it from Casey, who saw them there."

Virginia frowned. Greg Smith was the number-one-most-popular-guy at Fairview High. *If I'd gone out with him, I would have told everybody in the state.* "What about you, Sam?" Mr. Stevens asked. "Have you anything to add?"

Sam scratched his head. "I really don't know Kim very well at all. She never talks about her family—I don't even know if she has brothers or sisters."

"Me either," Virginia said. *How can you work next to someone every day, and know so little about them?*

"Why are you asking us all these questions," Jo demanded. "Is there something wrong? Did Kim run away? Or was she—kidnapped?"

"Has anyone responded to the posters?" Virginia asked.

Ms. Denson exchanged a look with Mr. Stevens, who took a deep breath. "Kim's car was found smashed against a tree in Lyon Park."

"Lyon Park?" Trip repeated. "In the center of town?"

Ms. Denson nodded.

"How could her car be there?" Virginia asked. "We were all over that park on Saturday putting up posters."

Ms. Denson looked at her closely. "The car was—hidden in some brush. Difficult to detect."

"Oh." Virginia wanted to ask more but was cut off by Mr. Stevens. "We believe she may have been running from something," he said, with a frown. "There was a change of clothes in the car, and some items which led her parents to believe she was upset and frightened."

"Yeah. I know how she feels," Trip said. "I've got a calculus test tomorrow with Mr. Cooney. Let me tell you, I'm tempted to run away, too."

"Kim hasn't run away," Mr. Stevens said, his frown growing even more severe as he stared grimly at Trip.

"Then why don't you ask her these questions?" Casey asked. "If her car was wrecked in the park, she couldn't have gotten very far on foot."

"We can't do that." It was Ms. Denson who spoke. "You see, Kim was found behind the wheel of her car. Dead."

chapter 5

*D*ead.

Virginia stared at her reflection in the mirror of the bathroom. She wiped her eyes again and tossed the tissue in the trash. Crying had always helped before when she felt out of control. But it wasn't helping this time. She couldn't believe it. Kim was dead. All of them had been stunned by the announcement. Then they'd fallen apart. Even Trip. Jo was so upset, Ms. Burns had to take her home.

The door to the bathroom opened and Casey came in. Tears shone on her eyelashes. "I just can't believe it. I just can't believe she's dead," Casey whimpered. "I feel so awful. A car accident. A stupid car accident."

"Why do you think they were asking us all those questions in the office?" Virginia asked. It bothered her that they'd been called into the office and given the third degree about Kim.

Casey turned toward the mirror to fix her makeup. Her mascara had left two dark smudges on her cheeks. "Maybe they just wanted to know her . . . her state of mind before she died." Casey shot Virginia a concerned look. "Maybe they think it was a suicide."

Virginia frowned. "But then why did she have a change of clothes with her?"

Kim can't be dead. Friday. I saw her Friday. I yelled at her.

"Maybe she was running away and—and she was so upset she went off the road."

Upset about our argument. I pushed her too hard and now she's dead. Virginia felt her eyes welling up again and she bit her lip hard, trying to hold back the tears.

Casey dabbed her cheeks with a wet paper towel. "I can't believe they expect us to go to back to class."

Virginia nodded. "Unfortunately, we have to start our story assignments for the next issue of the *Spectator.*"

"The *Spectator?*" Casey shook her head. "Is that all you ever think about? Deadlines and assignments for that newspaper?"

Virginia stared at the floor. "It helps me not think about Kim," she murmured. "That's how I cope."

She heard Casey sigh loudly, then felt her hand on her arm. "I'm sorry, I didn't mean to sound like a jerk," Casey said gently. "This is all so upsetting."

Virginia swallowed hard and tried to smile. "That's okay. I understand."

"Before I forget." Casey rummaged through her backpack. "I found a list of names of the basketball team. It was on the back of a game program. Here." She thrust the paper in Virginia's hand and hurried out of the bathroom.

Virginia stared at the paper.

That's right. The list. The picture. The knife in the door. How had everything gotten so weird?

Virginia stepped out into the hall. She could tell by the expressions on the faces of the passing students that word of Kim's death had spread. Compared to the usual hundred-decibel roar, the hall was almost silent. Another wave of sadness washed over Virginia and she could barely move.

Brrring.

The bell rang, signaling the start of another class period. But still she didn't move. Virginia stared down at the list in her hands. *Concentrate on that. You'll feel better.*

A few of the names were familiar—Matthew Harrison, Cody Jenkins, Troy Lennon, Skip Parker, and Will Manning. The five big stars of the basketball team. Now and then she remembered hearing about Steve Price and Joe Hayden. But the other two names—Adam Fellows and Jeff Clayton—she had no idea who they were.

Virginia frowned. Would any of these guys slice up a picture of their own team? And why? It was more likely that someone who hadn't made the team would have done the cutting.

"Virginia? Virginia!"

Virginia looked up, startled. Ms. Burns was standing directly in front of her. "I'm sorry, Ms. Burns. I didn't see you. I was thinking about something else."

The adviser's face was drawn with sadness, her eyes puffy and red—rimmed. "We might as well forget trying to get the story assignments done today," Ms. Burns said. "The sophomores are distributing the new issue, so we can wait a day or two before setting up articles."

"Is Jo okay?" Virginia asked.

Ms. Burns shook her head. "We're all shaken up." She gave Virginia a puzzled look. "Jo tells me you argued with Kim on Friday. Is that true? She said she overheard you."

Virginia blinked in surprise. "Kim hadn't finished the letters for the column and she was leaving the school grounds. I told her she needed to meet the deadline. I wouldn't call that an argument. A disagreement, maybe."

That sounds lame. Especially since Jo probably heard every word. But where was Jo? Was she the one in the bungalow?

"I wouldn't want to think you were taking your job as editor too seriously, Virginia. If you upset Kim—"

"It was a disagreement," Virginia cut in. Her voice was pinched with emotion. "A simple argument. That's all. No one would kill themselves over an argument."

"Kill themselves?" Ms. Burns frowned at Virginia. "Where did you get that idea?"

"I thought that since Mr. Stevens was asking all those questions about how Kim was feeling and acting, you must have thought it was a suicide."

Mrs. Burns shook her head, tears springing to her eyes once more. "No. Not a suicide. Maybe something far worse."

Virginia's eyes widened. "What do you mean, far worse?"

Ms. Burns waved her palm in the air. "Forget I said that. I'm upset. We all are." She pressed her hand to her mouth and took a shaky breath. "Don't worry about the paper for now, Virginia. We'll get to work on the next issue later."

Ms. Burns hurried away, and Virginia moved stiffly to her next class.

Not a suicide? Then it was an accident. A stupid accident. Does Ms. Burns think I'm responsible? It can't be my fault. Kim was upset before I saw her. Upset with someone in the newsroom.

The whole day passed like a terrible dream, with thoughts of Kim swirling in her brain. Mr. Cottle, her art teacher, had to call on her three times to explain the difference between abstract and cubist painting. Mrs. Farley practically fainted when Virginia told her she'd left her biology assignment in her locker. And she tripped and skinned her knee walking home from school. She was relieved when she finally stepped up onto the front porch of her house.

Unfortunately, Virginia had barely taken off her coat when the doorbell rang.

"I'll get it," she called to her mother, who was upstairs.

Virginia opened the door. There stood Trip and Sam, looking cold and uncomfortable.

"What are you guys doing here?" she asked, ushering them into her living room.

Trip sat on the oriental rug, his back against the couch. "Things are getting weird, Virginia. Sam here—well, you tell her, Sam."

Sam perched on the straight-backed chair across from Trip. "I was going through my computer files before I left school, checking on my series about the school clubs. Remember I was starting with the Science Club?" He paused, annoyance flashing across his face.

"And?"

"The article's gone."

"What do you mean, gone?" Virginia crossed her arms in front of her.

"The article was wiped out."

"You mean you erased it?" Virginia asked.

"Negative." Sam raised one finger. "I didn't erase it. I know it was there this morning. Someone else nuked it. And they took my backup disk."

"Are you sure?" Virginia looked from Trip to Sam, and back to Trip.

Trip shrugged. "No one is more careful than Sam about his computer files. You know that."

"I couldn't have nuked it," Sam added emphatically. "It's just not possible."

"Maybe someone else used your computer station and trashed the article by mistake. Or maybe you named it something else," Virginia suggested, leaning forward in her chair. "Saved it in another file."

Sam pressed his fingers to his forehead. "That's possible. But I've never done anything like that, Virginia. I always write down what I name all my files and where I put them."

"But we were all upset . . . about Kim," Virginia said, softly. "Maybe you erased it while you were thinking about . . . her. And perhaps you just misplaced your disk."

Sam looked at his hands. "I know I was—am—upset. We all are. But I also know I would never do something so lame."

"There's more." Trip stood up and started to pace around the living room. "I got the Honor Roll list for the next issue from the office this morning. I laid it on my desk, then went to class. When I went back to get it, it was crumpled up and in the trash."

"Take that, my files, the sliced-and-diced photo, and the matte knife in the door," Sam said, ticking the items off on his fingers, "and we've got a major case of sabotage."

Virginia blew her bangs off her face. "I've been thinking about the photo. Do you think it's possible that someone could have been trimming an ad, and the photograph just happened to be underneath?"

Trip flopped down on the couch. "I guess. But we're all so careful about that. Especially since Jo sliced up that picture of the alumni party in September."

"That's true," Virginia agreed. "We've all made mistakes. Plenty of them."

"But never this many at one time," Sam pointed out.

"Besides, what about Kim?" Trip asked, leaning forward

A cold feeling slid up Virginia's spine. "What do you mean?"

"Why did they drag all of us into the office? Why didn't they investigate the crash and then just tell us about it? And the woman in the suit."

Trip's face creased into a confused expression. "Who was she, anyway?"

"Ms. Burns said she works with the police," Sam answered.

"Police!" Trip's eyes widened. "That's heavy. I mean, Mr. Stevens did mention that Kim's car was hidden under some bushes. What was that about?"

"Trip, do you have those pieces of the picture?" Virginia asked. "If we start with the first strange incident, maybe we'll find some sort of a connection."

Trip's blue eyes flashed. "Between Kim's death and the stuff that's been going on in the newsroom?"

Virginia shrugged. "You never know. I mean, everything is so bizarre."

Trip grabbed a white envelope from his backpack and dumped the pieces of the photo on the rug.

Sam leaned forward to look at them. "You're right, Trip. This is no accidental slicing. Here, let's put it together." Sam spread the pieces out flat, and they all began assembling them like a jigsaw puzzle.

Virginia added a face to a body, Trip stuck in

an arm and a leg, and when they were done, the three of them stared at what they had put together.

"Part of it's missing," Virginia said.

"Can you tell who it is?" Trip asked, squinting at the photo.

Virginia pulled her list of names out of her purse. "Here. I got this from Casey. It's a roster of the players."

Trip grinned. "Very efficient, Virginia. Let me see it."

Virginia handed it to him, scooting closer so she could see both the list and the pieces. "Okay, there's Matthew Harrison."

Sam peered at the photo. "Check. He's there."

Trip read the list and Sam checked the faces of the picture. "Cody Jenkins. Troy Lennon. Steve Price. Joe Hayden. Will Manning."

Sam studied the faces glimmering from the glossy print. He pressed the edges together. "I think that is part of Jeff Clayton's face."

"Yeah, you can't miss it. He looks like Godzilla," Trip added.

Virginia scanned the list. "That leaves Adam Fellows and Skip Parker." She looked up at Trip.

"If you give me the Honor Roll, and Sam, you get me a list of the Science Club members, then I can compare them and see if there are any names in common."

Sam nodded. "And if there are, we have to figure out what that could possibly have to do with Kim."

"It'll be on my desk first thing tomorrow," Trip said, standing up. Sam got up as well and Virginia led them to the front door.

They stepped out onto the porch and were headed down the front steps when Sam turned toward her. "Oh, I almost forgot." He rummaged in his jacket pocket and drew out a wrinkled letter. "This was in the Incoming Heart-to-Heart box. I heard the box lid creak open while I was looking for my files, but I didn't see who put it in there. I thought you'd like to see it. It's marked Top Secret."

"Thanks." As Virginia took the letter, a shiver of apprehension rippled through her.

The boys crunched through the snow toward Sam's old Mercury. "Make sure you don't lend your Bungalow key to anyone," Virginia called after them. "We need to keep a tight rein on who goes in and out."

"Right." The boys hopped in the car and zoomed away, leaving a large cloud of blue smoke behind them.

Virginia stepped into the light on her porch and ripped open Desperate's envelope.

Dear Heart,

Dingdong the witch is dead. Now she calls the grave her bed. She did us all a favor.

Happy?

"Oh, my God," Virginia moaned, dropping the letter as if it were on fire. "This person is a total sicko."

chapter 6

Watch out, Virgo—your Moon is in Scorpio, a very powerful conjunction that could stir up emotions you never thought you had. Could Cupid be aiming that arrow at you? Don't push too hard—emotions are tricky and Venus is as fickle as she is beautiful.

Virginia stood by the Outgoing box outside the Bungalow and studied the note she'd written the night before. It was terse and to the point.

Dear Desperate,
I'm not happy about Kim. Don't write to me anymore.
You're very sick. Get professional help, now.

Heart

She dropped the note in the box, then unlocked the newsroom door. Virginia had a mission. Trip had said he would leave the Honor Roll on his desk first thing Tuesday morning.

The bell for third period rang as Virginia let herself into the newsroom office. She flicked on the heat, hung up her jacket, and got out the basketball team list.

She hurried to Trip's desk. Where was the Honor Roll? Trip said it had been crumpled up, which would make it easy to spot. She flipped through his sketches and articles. If she compared the names from the Honor Roll list with those from the basketball team, maybe she'd see a relationship. But the Honor Roll wasn't there.

"What are you looking for?"

Virginia spun around. Emily stood there, her overcoat in her arms. She hadn't made a sound. She looked like an old-fashioned painting in her rose-print dress, with cotton mauve tights and ankle-high leather boots.

"Oh, Emily! You startled me." Virginia gestured at the scattered papers on the desk. "I'm looking for a list Trip said was on his desk. But I can't find it."

Emily crossed to her computer and pulled off the cover. When she tossed it onto Jo's workstation, Virginia noticed a gauze bandage on the palm of Emily's hand.

"What's with my newspaper staff?" Virginia asked. "Is everybody accident-prone or something?"

Emily looked confused for a minute. Virginia pointed to her hand. "Oh, my hand," Emily replied. "I tried to pick up a broken water glass, and some of it sliced my hand."

"Don't you have a class this period?" Virginia asked.

"Independent study. I thought I'd use this time to get a head start on the horoscopes. I usually try to get them finished by Wednesday. But tomorrow's the funeral. You know school's been canceled."

A wave of sadness washed over Virginia. "That's right. Poor Kim."

Emily immediately set to work typing, then paused with her fingers over the keys. "Looks like it's romance on the horizon, Virgo," Emily said, turning slightly. "All the charts say so. Every one."

Virginia gave Emily a doubtful glance. "That proves it. There's nothing to those horoscopes. They just write what people want to hear."

Emily shrugged. "Maybe."

Sam came in the door, waving two disks in

the air. "Whoever dumped my files is in for a big surprise."

"Don't tell me you had extra backups." Virginia knew Sam was careful about his files, but *double* backups?

Sam nodded. "I never trust my work to one or even two backup disks. Too many people use these machines. So whoever killed my article will have a heart attack when it appears in the next issue."

Sam slid into his chair at the computer and plugged in a disk. The computer whirred and pretty soon columns of text appeared on the screen. "Ta da!"

"Could I have a hard copy of it?" Virginia asked. "I can keep the articles at home. That way they'll be sure to be safe."

"Good idea, Virginia. I'll print one out right away."

A soft creak could suddenly be heard from outside. It sounded at first like the boards of the old building contracting in the cold but as Virginia listened, she realized it wasn't that at all. It was a hinge. The hinge on the Heart-to-Heart box.

She made a run for the door, flinging it open in time to see a slim, yellow-haired girl dressed in black standing next to the delivery boxes.

When she saw Virginia, she jerked her hand out of the box and fled.

Virginia hurried over to the box, flipped open both lids, and peered inside. Both empty. The girl must have taken her response and then changed her mind about leaving a letter. But that didn't matter.

That must have been Desperate. Now if I can just find out her name.

Virginia's pulse raced with excitement. She raced back into the Bungalow to the window, through which she could still glimpse the blonde girl as she crossed the quad. "Sam, do you know who that is?"

Sam squinted out the window. "Alice Monroe, I think. A sophomore. She's in our Spanish class, isn't she, Emily?"

Emily leaned back to look. "Yes. That's Alice."

"Do you know anything about her?" Virginia asked.

"Not much. She's kind of quiet," Emily said. "And strange. She refuses to answer questions in class. She won't practice the conversational drills with her partner. Señora Hunter has pretty much given up on getting her to do anything. She's . . . sullen."

Sam nodded. "Yep. That's how I'd describe Alice."

Sullen? Strange? That sounds like Desperate.

"Alice Monroe." Virginia said the name out loud. *I caught her at the letter box. She was acting suspicious. But she seems so meek. It's hard to believe she could write so cruel a letter.*

The printer was clattering out a copy of Sam's article when Trip walked in the door.

"Trip, I've looked everywhere for the Honor Roll list," Virginia called. "I can't find it."

"Oh, sorry." He unzipped his backpack and peered in. "I stuffed it in here by mistake."

Virginia took the list and sat down at her desk to compare it with the basketball team roster.

"I think we should do a special article on Kim," Trip said, slumping in his chair. "I'm sure Ms. Burns would allow us to print a tribute on the front page."

Virginia smiled at him sadly. "That's a wonderful idea. We could interview her friends, even put together several memorials."

Casey hurried into the newsroom. "Hello, everybody." She dumped her backpack onto the couch and moved to the filing cabinet.

"Casey," Virginia called, "do you have any file pictures of Kim we could run in a tribute?"

She shook her head. "Nope. I used to have lots. Like I told Mr. Stevens, she wanted them, so I gave them to her." Casey squinted one eye shut. "Wait a minute. I should have her in a few group shots." Casey flipped through the files quickly. "That's odd."

"What is?" Virginia rose and crossed to the filing cabinet.

"They're gone, too."

Virginia peered over Casey's shoulder at the drawer of files. "Are you sure?"

"Yeah. There was one with the Chess Club, and one with the concert choir. But both of them are missing."

"I might have one or two at home you could use," Emily said. When Casey and Virginia turned to look at her, a slight flush stole up her cheeks. "I don't have the photos you're looking for but I do have a few photos I took myself. On Back-to-the-'60s Day. Remember?"

"Oh yeah." Casey nodded, flipping the files shut and slamming the drawer. "She wore that East Indian vest with little mirrors on it. It had those cool beads all over it, too. Nice outfit."

"That's right," Emily said. "I snapped some pictures of her as she came to school."

"Here you go, Virginia." Sam pulled the copy of his Science Club information out of the printer and handed it to her. She scanned it quickly, comparing it with the basketball team and Honor Roll lists, and immediately two names jumped off the page.

Skip Parker and Adam Fellows.

Skip was a tall gangly boy who lived to play basketball. But he was a brain, too, and always made the Honor Roll. He hung out with the athletes and now and then smiled at her in the hall. And Adam Fellows? She'd seen his name a few times but had no idea who he was or what he looked like.

The bell rang, and as the rest of the staff left the Bungalow for the lunchroom, Virginia reached for her textbook on English and Romantic poetry. The letter she'd tucked inside the day before slipped out and fell on the floor. Another one was with it. From Desperate.

Not another letter. I don't want to ever think of her again.

Virginia had picked up the computer paper and started to crumple it into a small ball when the last few words caught her eye.

He's disappearing slowly. First his name. Then his face. Soon he'll be gone without a trace.

It was a threat. Virginia's knees suddenly felt weak and she collapsed into her chair as the pieces fell into place.

". . . disappearing slowly. First his name," she said out loud. *The Honor Roll list and the Science Club article.* "Then his face." *The basketball team photo.* "Soon he'll be gone without a trace." *Oh, my God. Maybe Desperate plans to hurt this boy. But who is he?*

Virginia's hands were shaking as she searched for the two names she'd written down and tucked in her purse. "Skip Parker and Adam Fellows."

Her mind was racing a million miles a second— almost as fast as her heart was pounding. A possible scenario took shape in her mind. Maybe Desperate was jealous. Skip or Adam, one of them dumped her. She got angry and sabotaged the newsroom. If she could do all that just to get back at this boy, then she really might follow through with her threat to make him disappear without a trace. She was definitely cold-blooded enough to do it. *Look at the note she wrote about Kim.*

Virginia stood up and hurried to the door. "I've got to find Skip and Adam and warn them. Now."

chapter 7

Usually, the lunchroom roared with chattering voices and the crash of trays and plates. But today the students sat quietly at their places, murmuring to each other. Occasionally one of the girls would wipe her eyes. Even the cafeteria staff looked glum. Outside the big double-paned windows, dull gray clouds scudded across the sky.

Virginia spotted Skip Parker with a bunch of athletes across the room. He was stuffing forkfuls of meat loaf into his mouth as he talked.

As she neared the table, several of the boys stared at her, and a hot flush stole up her cheeks.

"Skip?" Virginia said in a stiff, nervous voice. "May I talk to you?"

The athlete, who was about six feet four and built like a telephone pole, looked up at her in surprise. "Sure, Virginia," Skip answered. "Is it for the paper?"

"Uh, yes. Something like that. Could we talk over here?" She gestured toward an empty table, and Skip shrugged. "Sure."

"Why not talk out back?" the guy beside him said, poking him in the ribs. "It's more private there."

Virginia felt her blush deepen as the other boys leered and winked at her.

"Get a life," Skip called over his shoulder as he carried his food-laden tray over to the next table. He sat down facing Virginia. "So what's on your mind?"

Virginia felt like everyone in the lunchroom was staring at them, but she couldn't let that bother her. "It's really sad about Kim, isn't it?" she began.

Skip nodded as he chewed a piece of meat loaf. "Sure is. I didn't know her. My girlfriend did, though, and she says she was really nice."

"You didn't know her?" Virginia knit her eyebrows in confusion. "At all? But she goes to this school."

He shrugged. "Sorry. I know what she looked like and all. But we didn't have any classes together."

Virginia frowned as the other half of what he'd just told her sank into her head. "Girlfriend? You have a girlfriend?"

"Yeah," he said with a smile. "Kathy McCormick. We've been going steady for two years this February. Know her?"

"Everyone knows Kathy. She's a cheerleader," Virginia replied. "Congratulations on two years."

He took a huge bite of meat loaf. "Thanks. We're planning on lasting even longer. We've both been accepted at KSU."

Well, that shoots the jealous-girlfriend theory. He and Kathy are obviously doing just fine.

Virginia looked around at the other kids in the lunchroom. *I'm probably the only person in this room who didn't know Skip and Kathy were going steady. I am totally out of it. Might as well hang a sign over my head that says* ISLAND.

"Kathy has a different lunch period than I do," Skip said, watching Virginia closely.

"Oh, of course." Virginia stood up. "Well, thanks for talking with me." Her mind was instantly focused on the other name on the list, the boy she didn't know at all. If Skip Parker had a steady girlfriend, that meant Adam Fellows was the boy she needed to talk to.

Skip waved his fork in the air. "But you didn't ask me anything yet. Did you want to know about our next game or not?"

"Oh, yeah." Virginia dug in her purse for a notepad and pen. "What do you think about the Grizzlies' chances of beating the Vikings this Friday night?" Virginia knew it sounded lame, but she couldn't think of anything original.

"The Vikings are going to eat the Grizzlies' shorts."

"Great quote," Virginia said, pretending to write it down.

Skip looked pleased. "Will my picture be in the paper?"

"We'll see." She rose to leave. *Picture. This would be a good chance to ask Skip about the other missing team member.*

"Uh, Skip? Could you point out Adam Fellows to me?"

Skip smiled at her smugly. "Sure."

He must think I'm desperate for a date or something.

Skip glanced around the crowded room, then

shook his head. "This is Adam's lunch period. But I don't see him. He's not here. Sorry."

"Oh. Thanks anyway for your help."

"Sure." Skip picked up his plate and returned to his table.

"Watch out, man," one of the beefier guys chided. "Kathy's gonna be steamed."

"Hey, Skip, I didn't know you played the field," another cracked.

"Shut up, you bozo." Skip flicked some mashed potatoes at the boy next to him, who flipped a few peas back at Skip. Virginia could see this was the beginning of a full-fledged food fight but she had no desire to stick around and find out who was going to win. She had to track down Adam Fellows. But how? *I don't even know what he looks like.* Virginia moved down the hall, trying to think of a plan for finding Adam. As she approached the main office, a student hurried out of the door carrying a hall pass and a voice sounded from inside.

"Fairview High School, may I help you?"

Mrs. Lennox! She'd ask the secretary for Adam's schedule. She rushed into the office and stood on the other side of the broad counter. "Excuse me?" Virginia smiled her friendliest smile.

Mrs. Lennox cocked her head to one side and smiled back. "Yes, dear?"

"I wonder if I could get a student's schedule?"

Mrs. Lennox frowned. "We usually don't give out schedules, Virginia. It's against school policy."

"But—but I have to talk to a student for a newspaper article. It's really important." She flashed Mrs. Lennox her most convincing I'm-a-conscientious-student-and-would-never-do-anything-wrong smile.

"All right. As long as it's for the paper. But you should try to arrange these things in advance, you know. Who is the student?"

"Adam Fellows."

Mrs. Lennox rose and crossed to the counter. She flicked through the collection of student schedule cards, pulled one out, and quickly copied the classes onto a blank card. She handed it to Virginia.

"There you are. Try to set up your interview during a free period, if you can. The teachers would appreciate it."

Virginia took the card and gave Mrs. Lennox another brilliant smile. "I'll remember. Thank you so much."

"You're welcome, dear."

Virginia rushed out the door and stopped to read the card. Patterson's world history, then English. Last period free. She hurried down the hall and turned the corner toward the history classrooms. She decided go to Mr. Patterson's room and wait outside in the hall. Maybe she could catch Adam before he went into class.

The bell rang and she watched as the hall filled with students. Hundreds of feet thumped along the tiles; lockers banged; backpacks rustled. One by one, the world history students filed past her into the classroom.

"Hey, Virginia," Kirk Boyd called as he passed her. "What's up?"

She grabbed him by the arm. "Kirk, I need you to point out Adam Fellows to me. I want to interview him."

"Forget Adam. Who's Adam?" Kirk joked. "Do a story on me. I was once kidnapped by aliens."

"You *are* an alien," Virginia shot back.

The students around them laughed, and Virginia smiled. Then Troy Lennon bumped into her while rummaging in his backpack for some papers. He was a member of the basketball team. He'd know Adam.

"Troy," Virginia asked, "is Adam Fellows here? He's in this class, isn't he?"

Troy gave her a nod, then peered around at the thinning crowd of kids in the hall. He ducked his head into the classroom and then leaned back out. "He's in this class, but I don't see him. Sorry."

As Troy stepped into the class, Mr. Patterson made an announcement. "The test Friday will cover chapters six through ten in the textbook. I will also expect you to remember . . ."

His voice faded away as he closed the door.

Virginia frowned, studying the schedule card in her hand.

Not at lunch. Not in history. Where is he?

She headed back down the hall. What if Desperate had already done something terrible to Adam, and nobody knew it? She had to find out.

Mrs. Neumann, the French teacher, came out of the faculty lounge and stared at her. "Virginia? Aren't you supposed to be somewhere?"

Virginia flinched. "Oh, yeah. I guess I am."

"Then I suggest you go there immediately."

"Right."

Virginia headed back to the main office. When she came through the double doors again,

Mrs. Lennox looked up at her and smiled. "Back so soon? How did the interview go?"

"Well, I'm a little frustrated, Mrs. Lennox. I can't seem to find Adam Fellows. He's not in any of his classes. I wonder if I could have his address?"

Mrs. Lennox shook her head. "Now, that really *is* against school policy. There's even a law against it, you know."

"There is? But——but my deadline for this article is Thursday. And with the funeral . . ." She didn't have to pretend to be depressed about it. The thought of Kim's funeral made her stomach feel like it had been turned to stone.

Mrs. Lennox pursed her lips. "Oh, all right. Since it's you, Virginia. I know you won't be harassing him or anything like that. But we do have to be careful these days. Let me get it for you." The secretary once again rose from her desk and crossed to the row of filing cabinets lining the wall of the office. She grabbed a piece of paper, jotted down the address, then handed it to Virginia.

As she left the office, Virginia glanced at the slip of paper. *750 Harrison Street. That's only four blocks away from my house.*

Jahnna N. Malcolm

Three long hours of school remained. Virginia spent every minute of them in agony, worrying about Adam. When the last bell finally rang, she was the first one out of the building.

chapter 8

Virginia hurried down Harrison Street as the clouds settled into a solid gray mass across the sky. The wind had picked up since morning and now blew cold, damp air into her face. She clutched the slip of paper in her shaking fingers.

She couldn't believe how nervous she was. The interview with Skip had gone okay. *Of course, he probably thinks I'm a total nutcase. He's probably telling his friends Virginia Wells has totally lost her mind.*

Following the curve of the street, Virginia checked house numbers.

738. 748. Ah—750.

She stood for a moment on the sidewalk, surveying the large white two-story house with the wide front porch. How normal it seemed. It didn't look like anything horrible had happened there. She hurried up the stairs, shivering when a blast of wind sailed down the collar of her jacket.

She pushed the doorbell.

Dingdong.

A flurry of excited voices erupted inside.

"I'll get it!"

"No! It's my turn."

"I want to answer the door!"

"Take a hike, Cameron. I'll get it."

The door opened suddenly, and Virginia's jaw dropped open.

The boy standing in front of her was tall, a little over six feet, with broad shoulders. On the thin side, but he still gave the impression of solid strength. He had dark brown hair, a wide smile, and a straight nose. And his eyes! They were the color of a tropical bay, like in the travel magazines, all light and sea green.

I must have the wrong address. This guy couldn't go to Fairview High. I would have noticed him. Everyone *would have noticed him!* She continued to stare at him, speechless. The boy laughed as two small children, one about five and the other roughly six, peered out from behind his legs.

"Excuse me," Virginia finally stammered. "I must have the wrong house. I was looking for Adam Fellows."

A pleased look flashed across the boy's face. "No, you don't have the wrong house," he said in smooth voice that had a slight Southern accent. "I'm Adam."

"You are?" She could feel a blush rise from her neck to her forehead. "You—you go to Fairview High School?"

He nodded slowly. "Last time I checked."

"I've never seen you before," Virginia blurted out, like a total idiot.

"I've seen you," he replied. "In the lunchroom."

Virginia suddenly remembered her mission, and she put on her best formal voice. "I'm sorry to disturb you at home. I was working on an article and—and I wanted to talk to you."

The kids behind Adam's legs giggled. "Hey, Diane, Cameron, give me a break," he told them affably. "You're cutting off the circulation in my legs." The kids stayed glued to his thighs.

Virginia tucked a strand of hair behind one ear. "I'm Virginia Wells, editor of the *Spectator*, and I wondered if I might ask you a few questions about the basketball team?"

"You want to talk to me about the team?" Adam laughed a little and crossed his arms. "I'm the head benchwarmer, you know. I don't get to play much."

"That's okay. I'm trying to talk to everyone—" The wind gusted again, and her hair blew across her face. She pushed it out of the way.

"Would you like to come in? It's cold out there." Adam detached Diane and Cameron from his legs and escorted Virginia into the living room. "We're still unpacking boxes. But at least you can make it from room to room now. If you'd come over last week, you wouldn't have been able to see the floor."

As they settled themselves at opposite ends of the couch, Virginia studied the room. Floor-to-ceiling bookcases, crammed with books, framed the brick fireplace at the far end of the room. The sofa and chairs were of the over-stuffed floral variety, and the ancient coffee table had the telltale crayon marks which said that more than one child had used it to practice writing. The room felt cozy and comfortable.

"Scoot, you characters," Adam called to Diane and Cameron, who were still staring at Virginia as if hypnotized. The children giggled and darted out the door to the hall. Then they stuck their faces back around the jamb and giggled some more.

"Excuse the leeches," Adam said, waving them away. "They come with the house."

"They're cute," Virginia said, genuinely meaning it.

"So you want to ask me about the team?"

Virginia nodded, pulling her spiral pad and pen out of her purse.

"Well, I play quite a bit in practice, but watch a lot of games," Adam said with a shrug. "My parents thought it would be a good way to meet people." He smiled at her. "It isn't."

"Why not?"

"I've met the guys on the team, of course. But my time is so tied up with practices, games, and homework that I wouldn't be able to do anything with anybody even if I did get to know them. Do you know what I mean?"

"Yeah, I do know what you mean." It sounded to Virginia like he was too busy to have a girl-friend. How could he have had the time to make Desperate angry at him?

"I've met a few people," Adam continued. "But none of them seem to share my schedule at school."

"Where did you move from?"

"Georgia. We came up here in October."

"There she is," a soft voice said from the door. Virginia turned around and saw a little boy, about seven years old, staring at her. "Oooh, she's cute!"

"You kids, scram!" Adam leaped off the couch and chased the kids from the room, laughing when they screamed in delight. He pulled a sliding door shut, then moved back to the couch.

When he sat back down, he was still grinning. "Half-siblings. Diane, Cameron, and Harry. A whole gaggle of 'em."

"They seem to like you a lot." Virginia had heard plenty of kids at school talk about their stepbrothers and sisters as if they were one step up from carriers of the Black Plague. But not Adam. "And vice versa."

"Yeah. They're pretty cool." Adam leaned back against the soft couch. "My dad died when I was really young. When Mom remarried she started over again. Now I'm the big brother and head baby-sitter."

"Is that why you weren't in school today?"

Adam raised an eyebrow. "I was there all

morning but Mom needed my help this after-
noon so I left at lunchtime." He raised one hand.
"It was all aboveboard, I swear. I talked to Mr.
Patterson and everything."

Virginia blushed. "I guess I do sound like I'm
with Social Services. I was just curious—"

Thunk!

Something hit the door and Virginia started
in alarm. "What was that?"

This time it was Adam's turn to blush.
"Sounds like the kids are throwing their stuffed
animals at the door." He hopped to his feet. "You
know what? We're not going to be able to talk
here. Want to go somewhere else?"

Virginia nodded. *That will give me an opportu-
nity to focus my thoughts.* Ever since she'd seen
Adam, she seemed to be suffering from a serious
lack of concentration. *That's not like me at all.*

Adam hurried to the hall. "Hey, Mom!" he
called, pulling open the door. "I'm going out for
a while."

A woman's voice echoed from somewhere in
the back of the house. "All right!"

Adam grabbed a blue warm-up jacket with
the FAIRVIEW GRIZZLIES insignia across the back.
Within seconds they had climbed into his car,

had pulled out of the driveway, and were heading down the street.

"How about Ziggy's?" Virginia asked as they pulled out onto Fremont Street.

"Who, what?"

She laughed. "Ziggy's. It's a pizza place down on Jefferson. Most of Fairview High hangs out there. As long as we buy food, the owners don't seem to mind."

"Sounds good."

Adam deliberately didn't turn on the car radio. "Isn't silence great?" he asked, grinning at her. "I never appreciated it much before all the kids started appearing. Too much noise and I go brain-dead."

"Me, too. I guess I'm lucky. I get lots of quiet at home."

"Only child?"

She winced. "I know what you're thinking. Only children are spoiled and difficult."

"Hey, I was an only child for a long time, and I loved it," Adam replied. "I don't think anyone thought I was spoiled."

Or difficult. Virginia sighed as she looked at his handsome profile. *They were probably too busy thinking you were perfect.*

Virginia pinched herself. *Snap out of it. You have to ask him about his girlfriends. There must be plenty of them. Adam's probably lost track of all the girls he's dated since he moved here.*

She decided to start with the general and move to the specific. "Even if you don't have a lot of extra time, I bet you've made lots of friends at school."

"Not really," he replied. "I like the school a lot but it's a little hard to break into. I guess it's the same everywhere, but the popular kids here . . ." He groped for the right words. "They're a tight bunch. Seems like they really control who's in and out, and . . . well, you know."

"But you must have made some friends." *A gorgeous guy like you.*

Adam shrugged, apologetically. "The only person I knew for quite a while after I first moved to Fairview was my neighbor in the duplex next to us."

"When did you live there?"

"Until just before the New Year. We bought this new place at the end of December and moved in the first of January."

Virginia leaned her head back against the car seat. "Well, I've lived in Fairview my whole life, and I still think it's hard to meet people. If I didn't work on the school newspaper, I'd probably never meet anyone."

"I bet that's fun," Adam said, glancing at her. "Working on the paper, I mean. I wish I had done something like that instead of joining the basketball team."

"You should!" Virginia cried, sitting up. "We're picking a new staff next month. The adviser wants to sort of shake things up. It would be great to have you on the paper." *Calm down. You're gushing.*

Adam grinned. "I read the paper all the time. That editorial you did on the Student Council was really good. I even read the horoscopes."

"You do?"

"Yeah. Let's see, this month I'm supposed to meet a new friend and communicate on a new level."

"Oh." Virginia cocked her head. "You're a Leo."

Adam chuckled. "I guess you read them, too."

"Not as a rule. It's just that yesterday we were discussing them and Trip, he does our cartoons—"

"Oh, yeah, he's pretty weird. Good but weird."

"Well, Trip said that he was a Leo and that was his horoscope."

"Well, I don't know how Trip's doing, but so far, mine seems to be coming true." Adam grinned slyly at her and Virginia felt her cheeks grow warm with pleasure.

They smiled at each other as Adam pulled the car into Ziggy's parking lot.

Suddenly, she didn't want to talk about his girlfriends or threatening letters or anything unpleasant. *I'm having too good a time.*

Adam cruised slowly around the crowded parking lot, searching in vain for a space. "What is this? Grand Central Station?"

Virginia laughed. "It's pretty popular. There's a spot."

He pulled into a narrow parking slot, then climbed out and came around to her side of the car. He even took her elbow, as though he were really escorting her. It felt comforting and nice.

Virginia saw a flash of movement a couple of cars away. Someone with blonde hair. It was Alice Monroe, the sophomore Virginia had caught standing at the Heart-to-Heart box. As Alice passed Virginia and Adam on her way toward the entrance of the big, square brick building, she kept her eyes downcast.

"Hi, Alice," Virginia called, even though she'd never been formally introduced.

Alice barely looked up. "Hi, Virginia," she said. She kept her eyes glued to the ground until she reached the pizza parlor door.

Virginia narrowed her eyes. Alice hadn't seemed surprised to see Virginia or Adam. It almost seemed like the girl knew they'd be here at Ziggy's. Maybe Alice really was Desperate and had been watching Adam's house. Maybe she'd followed them.

"You want to go in?" Adam studied Virginia's face. "We don't have to, if you think it's too crowded."

Virginia snapped back to the moment. "No, no. I was just thinking about something." *Ask him. Now.* "Do you know Alice?"

"Only slightly," Adam replied, grabbing hold of the big wooden door handle.

Slightly. What does that mean?

Before Virginia could ask him to explain, he'd flung open the restaurant door and they were hit with a wave of sound and heat, and the delicious aroma of freshly baked pizza.

"Yo, Adam!" someone called from their left.

Trays clattered. A voice from the kitchen shouted, "Extra cheese on that Supreme!"

"Hey, Virginia!"

Trip, Sam, and Emily were in a booth to her left, stuffing slices of pizza in their mouths. Emily and Sam just looked at her, but Trip waved his limp pizza in her direction. "Over here!" he called.

Virginia signaled to Trip that she and Adam were going to sit somewhere else. She held up her spiral pad to show it was official business. Trip didn't seem to notice. He was dealing with the glob of cheese and tomato sauce that had fallen into his lap.

"Look, it's Virginia Wells. With a *boy*." Casey Collier's penetrating voice cut through the general restaurant noise. Virginia saw that Casey was sitting with the cheerleaders at a back table. "This is something I thought I'd never see."

Virginia shot a sideways glance at Adam to see if he'd heard Casey. *That would be too humiliating.* Luckily, he hadn't. Adam was preoccupied with asking a couple of kids near the telephone if the booth beside them was empty.

Virginia scanned the restaurant once more. It was amazing. The only person on her staff who wasn't there was Jo Plunkett. Virginia wasn't surprised. Jo had tried to come to school that morning but was sent home because she couldn't stop crying about Kim.

Toward the back of the main dining room, Alice sat alone at a table, staring at them.

"Let's sit over here," Adam said, guiding her toward the vacant booth, just around the corner.

"Fine with me." Virginia was glad to get out of the main traffic area. Too many eyes were staring at them.

They settled into the booth. While they waited for the waitress to show up, Virginia tried to order her thoughts so she could ask Adam about his social life. It seemed such an awkward way to start a conversation.

"Have you been to any of the dances at school?" she asked.

Adam opened his mouth to answer just as the waitress plunked two glasses of water in front of them. "What can I do for you?"

They ordered quickly and then Adam said, "No, I haven't, to answer your question." As he talked, he folded and refolded the corners of his place mat. "I always feel kind of strange walking into big groups when I don't know anyone."

"Me, too. Even when I know everyone, it feels strange."

Virginia was about to ask Adam about Alice and his ex-girlfriends when Trip appeared at their table. "Hey, Virginia. I asked Ms. Burns about the tribute to Kim. She thinks it's great. Since we can't find any pictures of her, I'm going to do some sketches."

Virginia nodded. "Good idea. Trip, this is Adam Fellows."

Trip shook hands with Adam. "Hi. I've seen you at the games."

"Yeah," Adam joked. "I have an important job—keeping the bench warm."

Trip grinned mischievously. "It's a tough job, but somebody's got to do it." Then he turned to Virginia once more. "I'll let you have the column measurements on Thursday."

"Okay."

Trip hurried back to his table, and Virginia looked at Adam. "I know you've heard about Kim Keller's death."

"Yeah." Adam shook his head somberly. "She was one of the few people I had actually met at this school. I couldn't believe it when I heard she was dead."

Now I'm getting somewhere. Virginia leaned forward. "So, you knew Kim? Did you two date?"

"No. It's funny how I met her. I was driving home from the store one day in December. It was really cold. Anyway, I noticed this girl standing beside an old, beat-up car by the side of the road. I stopped to see if she needed help. She did—her car had done a three-sixty on the ice and spun off the road. It must have hit something, 'cause she couldn't restart it. I gave her a ride. Kim was really nice."

Virginia nodded. "Everyone liked her. Besides being a nice person, she was an extremely valuable member of the newspaper staff. I'm going to miss her."

He nodded, staring off into the distance. It was very hard to believe that this boy, so sensitive and good-looking, didn't have a girlfriend. *He's got to. He's just not telling me about her.*

"So, if you didn't date Kim, who do you date?" Virginia practically shouted. Her hand flew to her mouth, and she felt herself turning scarlet. "I can't believe I said that! I mean—"

"I don't date anyone," Adam cut in with a laugh. "When we moved into the duplex on Carson Street, I only got to know the family next door. They were really nice and all, but then we moved into our house, and I haven't had time to strike up that kind of friendship." He smiled shyly at her. "Yet."

"Oh." Virginia couldn't believe her face could get any redder. But it did.

Luckily, the pizza came, and Virginia had time to regroup. She slid a piece of pizza onto her plate and busied herself with cutting it into smaller pieces.

Adam picked up a slice and took a bite. "I seem to have a ton of homework, and when I'm not doing homework, practicing layups at basketball practice, or watching the games from the bench, I'm baby-sitting the kids." He chuckled, then took another bite.

"I'm going to have to go to one of the games soon." She took a tiny bite of pizza, praying she wouldn't drip cheese all over her chin.

"Yeah. I'd like that. You could watch the back of my shirt."

The jukebox blared out the old Beatle song "Hey, Jude," and kids across the restaurant started singing along with the endless *na-na-na* part near the end. The waitresses and waiters joined in. Adam laughed and shook his head. "You're right about this place. It's really cool."

Shortly after the song ended Virginia noticed Trip, Emily, and Sam getting up from their table. They waved good-bye as they left the restaurant, and she waved back.

"So, who do *you* date?" Adam asked suddenly.

Virginia had just taken another bite of pizza, and she had to swallow quickly to keep from choking. "Uh, nobody."

"You're kidding me, right?" There was a playful glint in Adam's eyes, and a dimple appeared in his cheek as he smiled.

"No, I'm not. I mean, now and then I go on a date. But I don't date anyone steadily." *God, I sound like a major loser.*

Adam shook his head. "That blows me away. What are the guys around here—deaf and blind?"

Virginia fumbled with her napkin, pleased. Then a frown wrinkled her forehead. Adam wasn't the boy Desperate was trying to destroy. He couldn't be. He barely knew anyone at Fairview High, and he most definitely had not dated anyone.

Boy, am I glad I didn't mention the letters from

Desperate. He really would have thought I was a lunatic.

But if the notes weren't about him, who were they about? Whose face was sliced out of the basketball team's photograph? And who did Desperate want to disappear?

"Is something the matter?" Adam asked, studying her face.

"Yes. I mean, no." Virginia rearranged her napkin several times in her lap as she spoke. "It's just that, well, I think I have the wrong guy."

Adam gave her a long look, with more than a little sadness in it. "Story of my life," he muttered, and bit into his pizza.

chapter 9

Virginia sat up in bed. Something had awakened her, an unfamiliar sound. She stared, wide-eyed, into the darkness, listening.

A gust of wind hurled hail against her window. Virginia stumbled out of bed, groping across the room in the darkness. She always slept with a window open, even during the winter. Otherwise, she felt suffocated.

As she padded across the room in her bare feet, she shivered. The howling wind sounded almost like a voice, its pitch rising and falling eerily. Virginia put her fingers on the sash, then glanced quickly down into the front yard.

That's odd. She let her eyes focus on the front gate. *I'm sure that gate was closed when I came home.*

Now, it swayed open, its hinge squeaking. Black pools of shadow danced on the snow-covered yard. They shifted and trembled as the wind nudged the tree branches and shrubs.

Virginia was just about to turn back toward her bed when she caught sight of a pale light flickering in the bushes near the street. It was a thin trail of white, like a penlight, piercing the murky darkness.

Someone's out there!

Virginia stepped quickly back from the window, her heart pounding in her chest. *Who would be out in this snowstorm?*

She slowly peered around the window into the darkness once more. *You're just imagining things.* The weird incidents at the newsroom and the letters were starting to warp her imagination. Virginia surveyed the bushes one more time, then turned back toward her bed.

Crrreeeak.

That's the gate! Virginia wheeled back to the window. There, in the snow outside her fence, stood a figure dressed in black, with some kind of dark head covering. The figure shut the gate, then hurried away, the thin light of the flashlight fading along Madison Street.

Virginia's heart thumped painfully in her chest, and she felt a cold sweat rise along her spine. Someone had been out there. Watching her house. *Desperate!*

An intense feeling of immediate danger nearly overwhelmed Virginia. She could barely keep her hands from shaking as she quietly closed and locked her window.

I've got to tell Mom and Dad. And call the police! Virginia checked the clock by her bed. It was three-thirty in the morning. *Should I wake them?* Virginia stared again at the front gate and the dark bushes. Suddenly she wasn't sure if she had really seen anything at all. And if it had been an intruder, he or she was gone.

Virginia stood for a long time, looking out the window, trying to catch a glimpse of the dark figure again. Then the storm really picked up, making things look like the swirling interior of a glass paperweight. When she could finally see nothing but white, Virginia yawned. *I'm tired. And cold.*

She climbed back into bed, rubbing her feet together to warm them. *I'll talk to Mom and Dad tomorrow.*

———

Wednesday morning came too soon. Virginia rolled out of bed and shuffled to the window. The sun was obscured by hazy clouds. Everything was gray. The sky, the trees. Even the garden gate, now closed, cast a long gray shadow across the snow.

For some reason, a few lines from the end of Romeo and Juliet kept running over and over inside Virginia's head: "A glooming peace this morning with it brings. The sun for sorrow will not show his head."

Appropriate for the day of Kim's funeral. A lamentation for a girl and a boy who died too young.

Virginia showered and dressed. She didn't have anything black that was appropriate, so she wore a short navy-blue skirt and an oversized, maroon-and-blue-striped sweater. The whole time she was dressing, Virginia felt like she was moving through thick sludge.

Probably from lack of sleep. After last night . . . *What* did *happen last night? Was there really someone standing at our gate with a flashlight?*

"Virginia!" her mother called, interrupting her thoughts. "There's a note here for you."

Virginia frowned. A note? Who would be sending her notes? *Adam!*

She raced downstairs and took the envelope from her mother. It looked like—no, it couldn't be. But it was. The same kind of envelope Desperate used. And it was damp around the edges.

"From some admirer?" her mother asked with a suggestive wiggle of her eyebrows.

"I wish," Virginia grumbled. She took the envelope into the other room and slowly opened it, dreading what she might see written inside.

Stay away from him, bitch.
Or what happened to Kim will happen to you.

A cold wave of fear washed over Virginia. *Stay away from him?* Who? Adam?

It had to be Adam. But Adam said he didn't have a girlfriend. Unless he had lied to her.

. . . what happened to Kim will happen to you.

Virginia sat on the edge of the straight-backed chair and took three very deep breaths. Did this mean Desperate had something to do with Kim's death? Virginia's fear intensified, and her fingers trembled. If Desperate was responsible for Kim's death, and she left this note . . .

"Mom?" Virginia sprang out of the chair and hurried into the study.

"Hmmm?" Her mother was rearranging some papers in her briefcase.

"Where'd you find this note?"

"On the front porch, on the doormat. Listen, I'm heading out for a library board meeting this morning. Then I have lunch with Mrs. Swenson from work. Will you be able to get to the funeral all right?"

The funeral! In less than an hour Trip would be picking her up. "Um, yes. Trip McFadden is giving me a ride."

Her mother smiled. "He's a nice boy. A little on the strange side when it comes to humor, but nice." Her mother checked her watch. "I'd better run, honey, I'm going to be late."

"Okay." Virginia's voice caught in her throat. She knew she should tell her mother about the mysterious figure in the yard and this strange letter. *But what can Mom do? She's already late for a meeting. She'll just tell me to wait till this evening, "And we'll talk about it."*

Virginia followed her mother out to the front porch, where the note had been found. She

watched her walk to the gate, where she had
seen the dark figure.

She hurried back into the house to make a
cup of tea. Tea always made her think better. As
she heated the water and got the tea bag out of
the tin in the cupboard, Virginia tried to orga-
nize her thoughts. *Desperate must have seen me and
Adam at Ziggy's. She wrote the note and then crept
over here at three-thirty in the morning.* Virginia
paused with her teacup and saucer poised above
the counter. *In the middle of a snowstorm? She must
really be desperate.*

When the water boiled, Virginia poured it
over her tea bag and carried the delicate china cup
and saucer over to the breakfast table. Her father
had left for work early. The only sound in the
house was the ticking of the clock above the stove.

Desperate must be watching Adam constantly.
Virginia took a sip of tea and shivered. *Now she's
watching me. How creepy.*

Adam seemed so honest and straightforward.
Obviously, he must have broken up with
Desperate, was embarrassed about it, and didn't
want to tell her about it. *I don't blame him. He
barely knows me.*

"I need to talk to him." Virginia set her

teacup down firmly. "I'll tell him the situation and he'll come clean."

Reaching for the phone, she quickly dialed directory assistance, got Adam's number, and punched it into the phone.

One ring. Two rings. Three rings.

"Hi!" a very young voice piped.

"Hi. May I speak to Adam, please?"

"Ooooh, uuuuh, yeah." There was a pause, and Virginia could hear someone breathing into the phone. The phone clunked to the floor and then she heard more giggles.

"Is this . . . Diane?" Virginia remembered the two grinning faces peeking at Adam and her from the hall of his house.

"Uh-huh."

Virginia paused. At this rate, she'd never get ahold of him. "Listen, Diane. This is Virginia. I met you yesterday, remember? There's something really important I need to tell Adam. Could you please get him for me?" She made her voice sound like her preschool teacher, or at least what she remembered her preschool teacher's voice sounding like.

"Okay. But I don't know where he is."

"Is he at home?"

"He's—" The voice cut off, and a crackling sound crinkled through the line as someone else grabbed the receiver. "Hello? I'm sorry about that."

Just hearing his voice made Virginia a little weak inside.

She tried to put on her most professional manner. "Adam. This is Virginia."

"Hi there!" His voice cracked slightly and Virginia smiled at the receiver. "This is a nice surprise."

He sounded so genuine.

"Adam, there's something I need to tell you about the questions I was asking yesterday. Something I need to talk to you about."

"Okay," he said after a slight pause. "Shoot."

"Well, we've been having some . . . some very odd things happening at the newspaper. And I guess I didn't want to mention them at the pizza place."

"I understand. It was fun just getting to know each other."

"That's what I thought. But—but today . . ." She took a deep breath, and plunged in. "I think I need to tell you about them. Last Friday night, in the newsroom, Trip found a picture of the basketball team that had been sliced up with a knife."

"A rival team, you mean?"

"No. Ours."

"You're kidding."

"No, I'm not. Some—some of the faces were missing. And there were bloodstains on it."

"That's gruesome."

"You're telling me. We also found a matte knife stuck in the door. And Sam Calhoun . . . you know him, right?"

"Yeah, he's my Science Club partner."

"Well, his article about your club got deleted. Fortunately, he makes a zillion backups."

"Yeah, that's Sam, all right."

"Then, we had a list of the new Honor Roll students, and it ended up in the trash."

"What does this have to do with me?" Adam asked.

"Well, there were only two people who were in the photo, on the Honor list, and in the Science Club. You and Skip Parker."

"Uh-huh," Adam responded. "Skip's a good guy."

Virginia blew her bangs off her forehead in frustration. *He's not getting it.* "Listen, has anything strange or unusual been happening at basketball practice?"

"No, not unless you count me actually making a few baskets. That's pretty strange." He laughed a little. "But nothing creepy, if that's what you mean."

"Nobody's been watching you?" Virginia continued. "Or following you?"

"There are always people hanging around the gym, watching. But we don't get nasty notes or anything like that."

The notes. I should tell him about those. Virginia hesitated. She wanted to make certain he was the boy Desperate was talking about.

Virginia took another deep breath. "Adam, I'm going to ask you again. Are you sure you haven't dated anyone since you moved here?"

"I haven't dated a soul." Adam lowered his voice, sexily. "Except you, that is."

"Me?" Virginia felt her face turn pink.

"Well, we went out for pizza, didn't we? Some people might consider that a date."

"Yeah, I guess so, but—"

Beep-beep!

A car horn honked outside, and Virginia stretched the phone cord to peer out the kitchen window. Trip's car sat in her driveway.

"Oh, shoot! I've gotta go. Trip's here. He's driving me to the funeral. You're going, aren't you?"

"Of course."

Beep-beep!

"Oh, he's honking again." Virginia tapped on the window to catch Trip's eye. "He doesn't have to do that."

"Look, Virginia, why don't we talk after the funeral?" Adam suggested.

Beep-beep!

"Trip!" Virginia shouted in the general vicinity of the noise. "Stop honking." She turned back to the phone. "I think you're right. Let's talk later. After I kill Trip."

Adam chuckled softly. "I'll see you there, then."

"Right." Virginia started to hang up, then quickly pressed the phone back to her lips. "Oh, Adam? Adam, be careful, won't you?"

But he had already hung up. Virginia set the phone on its cradle and hurried into the hall to get her purse and coat. *Why didn't I just tell him about the note?* She caught sight of her reflection in the hall mirror. *Because you are a complete idiot when it comes to boys. They act nice to you and your brain turns to absolute mush!*

chapter 10

"**T**his is the first funeral I've ever been to," Trip mumbled as they pulled away from the curb. They headed south toward the church and cemetery, which were located on the far side of Fairview. His eyes were red-rimmed and he looked uncomfortable in his suit.

"Me, too," Virginia said. "I've never known anyone who died before."

Trip ran one hand through his hair. "I lay awake last night thinking about Kim. I just can't believe she was in Lyon Park. I mean right in the center of town. I put flyers on every tree and telephone pole in that park, Virginia. So did a lot of people. It's so weird that none of us saw her car."

"I know." Virginia pulled her wool coat around her and folded her arms across her chest to keep warm. "I've been wondering about that, too. A car right in the middle of a public park—how could we possibly miss it?"

"There is that road that runs through the trees," Tripped pointed out. "Where the gully drops off toward the creek. I guess that's where the car was. But it just doesn't make sense that nobody saw it. Maybe if someone had found it earlier—" Trip stopped. His chin wobbled and Virginia lay her hand on his arm.

"There's no sense thinking that way, Trip. It happened. It was awful. But it's over."

Trip looked sideways at Virginia. "I keep remembering the last thing I said to her." His voice cracked. "You see, she criticized my cartoon, so I told her to mind her own business. Or mind someone else's, but get out of my face." He squeezed his eyes shut, wincing. "I was having a bad day."

Virginia's eyes blurred with tears. "Oh, Trip. I had the same experience. Friday morning, she was leaving the Bungalow with a big box of stuff. I asked her where she was going and she wouldn't tell me. She looked really frightened and upset.

But what was I worried about? Our stupid newspaper deadline. I just kept harping about the Heart-to-Heart letters and the *Spectator*. She ran to the parking lot, screaming at me to leave her alone." Virginia hung her head miserably. "Maybe if I had been more understanding, she might not have gotten in that car. . . ."

Trip took her hand and squeezed it. "You were right. We can't think about that stuff. What's done is done."

When they reached the church, the parking lot was already full. Cars lined the streets outside the cemetery and in front of neighboring houses. "We may have to park a few blocks away," Trip said.

"That's okay. I could use the walk." Virginia was feeling a little shaky inside, thinking about that last morning with Kim. No matter what she did, she couldn't get that lingering image of Kim's face—pale, full of fear—out of her head.

The little white church was the oldest in Fairview. With its tall wooden steeple and simple construction, it looked like a New England postcard. As they approached the front steps, Virginia could hear Fairview's a cappella choir singing, "The silver swan, who living had no note, when death approached, unlocked her silent throat . . ."

Trip and Virginia stepped into the sanctuary. Both outer walls were lined with beautiful stained-glass windows and colored light spilled onto the students and teachers seated shoulder to shoulder in the pews.

In front of the altar sat a dark brown casket, its lower half covered with flowers. The top half was open. Virginia felt her throat tighten just looking at it.

Kim is in there. Inside that coffin.

Virginia spotted Jo off to the right, sitting near the aisle with Casey next to her, holding her camera on her lap. Virginia moved down the red-carpeted aisle and placed her hand on Jo's shoulder. "How are you doing?" she whispered.

Jo's spiky hair lay flat against her head and she wore a straight dark green dress. She looked up at Virginia with puffy red eyes. "Not good. I wanted to write something for Kim's tribute but I can barely pick up a pen."

"Give yourself time," Virginia murmured. "It's too difficult right now."

Casey, in a sleek black sheath, raised her camera. "I thought I'd take a picture of the flower arrangements." Her chin quivered. "But I am not taking a picture of that casket."

A tear trickled down Casey's cheek, and Virginia felt her insides go wobbly like Jell-O. She gave Casey's hand a squeeze and moved two pews ahead where Emily was signaling for her to join her.

"I wrote a poem to Kim," Emily whispered. "It's all in alexandrines and is two pages long. I think it should be our front page."

"Alexandrines," Virginia repeated mechanically. It was hard to think about the front page of the paper with Kim lying there so silent and cold before them. She patted Emily on the shoulder. "That's impressive. I think we'll talk about it—"

Suddenly she completely forgot what she was saying, because just then Adam walked into the church. In his dark brown suit and pale blue shirt, he was heart-stoppingly handsome.

How could I not have noticed him before? Virginia continued to stare at him, hoping to catch his eye. She had raised her hand to signal hello when someone touched her elbow.

"Miss Wells? May I speak to you for a moment?"

It was Ms. Denson, the counselor who worked with the police.

Virginia's stomach knotted. What was a police counselor doing at the funeral?

Ms. Denson led her into the back corner of the church, where a man in a dark blue suit stood waiting. "I want to give you this." She placed a shiny object in Virginia's hand. "It is yours, isn't it?"

Virginia looked down. Her grandmother's antique locket lay gleaming in her palm. "Where did you get this?" she whispered.

"It was in the back of Kim's car. She had a cardboard box full of items labeled with people's names. Your name was on this."

The same cardboard box Kim was carrying on Friday morning. "But how did Kim get it?" Virginia asked, fingering the chain nervously.

"Kim had your locket, Virginia, because she took it."

Virginia gasped. "What?"

Ms. Denson pursed her lips. "I'm afraid Kim had a problem with stealing. Her parents knew nothing about it."

"Kim took my locket?" Virginia was stunned. "Stole it?"

Ms. Denson nodded. "Chronic stealing can be a form of mental illness, you know. Sometimes people just can't stop themselves without professional help."

"I had no idea." Virginia closed her fingers over her grandmother's locket, her most treasured possession. "But I'm glad it's back."

"We're returning the other items to their rightful owners."

Virginia looked at her carefully, then at the man in the blue suit. "We?"

"I'm working with the police on the case," Ms. Denson replied. "Do you happen to know anyone who might have known about Kim's problem?"

Virginia wrinkled her forehead. "Maybe Jo Plunkett. They shared a locker, as you know. And they were friends. She did mention when we were in the office that Kim would change her outfits when she got to school." Virginia tilted her head. "Is that why Kim had such nice clothes? Because she stole them?"

"I'm afraid so. That way her parents never knew what was going on." Ms. Denson made a note on a small pad. "I'll talk to Jo. Anyone else?"

Virginia shook her head. "I can't think of anyone. Do you think Kim committed suicide because of her—her problem?"

Before Ms. Denson answered, she looked to the man from the police department, who nodded. "The evidence points to something else," Ms. Denson said. "As of this morning, the case is being considered a homicide." Ms. Denson touched her arm. "Thank you, Virginia."

"Homicide!" Virginia gasped. "You mean, murder?"

But Ms. Denson and the policeman had already moved away. The policeman went to a recess on one side of the church, where he could watch the entire congregation unobtrusively. Virginia watched as Ms. Denson went to the front pew and sat beside Mrs. Keller, who was sobbing into a handkerchief.

Kim was murdered. Virginia stumbled toward an empty space in the nearest pew, then sat down heavily on the cushioned seat.

Organ music began and the minister, clad in black robes, took his place in the pulpit. "Friends, we gather here today to say farewell to our friend, sister and daughter Kim Keller." His deep voice resonated through the church.

Virginia clasped her hands tightly in her lap, trying to absorb the news. Kim had been stealing from everyone and no one knew it. That explained Casey's missing film and pens. But what did that have to do with her death? And what about Desperate? Could that broken-hearted girl really have murdered Kim? Over a boy? And not just any boy. *Adam.*

Is Adam really who he says he is? He told her he didn't have a girlfriend and that he barely knew Kim. But if Desperate really murdered Kim because of Adam, then he had to be lying. Virginia stared down at her purse. *Maybe everyone lies about who they really are.*

After all, Kim had stolen from her friends, and Jo seemed to know nothing about it. Was Jo telling the truth? Or Casey? She'd acted like she was taking photos of the basketball game on Friday, but there she was in the parking lot, without her camera. Could she have sabotaged the newsroom and sliced up the photo? Could she be Desperate?

"Amazing grace, how sweet the sound . . ." Kim's favorite hymn swelled through the congregation and Virginia blinked at the students around her. She had been so lost in thought that she'd nearly missed the entire service.

The mourners, still crying and sniffing, rose and filed awkwardly into the center aisle. Virginia's arm was jostled as she struggled to grab a tissue from her purse. She lost her balance, but a hand came out to support her. She looked up. It was Adam.

He smiled sadly at her. "This was much tougher than I thought it would be."

Virginia nodded. She wanted to tell him about the threatening note, but they were squashed into the center aisle, the mass of people moving them forward as one.

Someone bumped them and Adam turned. "Hey, Casey." He bent down quickly. "You dropped your lens cap." He handed her the black plastic disk.

"Oh, thanks, Adam. I just can't believe how awful I feel." Tears streaked her cheeks and her nose was red.

The crowd surged forward once more, and Virginia gasped. They were at the casket. There was no escape. She'd have to walk past it.

Emily stepped next to Virginia. She was carrying a white rose.

"Hello, Emily," Adam said. "Is that from your garden?"

Virginia glanced at Adam quickly. How did he know Casey and Emily?

"All the roses are dead, Adam," she whispered. Then she gently placed the rose on Kim's coffin.

They moved past the burnished metal casket. Virginia glanced quickly at Kim, then turned away, tears stinging her eyes. *Sleeping. Kim looks like she's sleeping.*

Her vision blurred, Virginia felt Adam's comforting arm guiding her out of the church. They didn't speak, and before long she felt the cold air hit her face.

"You okay?" he whispered.

She nodded. "I—I didn't know you knew Casey and Emily," Virginia said, wanting to change the subject. Otherwise, she knew, she would break down completely.

He stood beside her in the churchyard, looking vaguely at the people walking toward the cemetery, which stretched beyond the parking lot across a rolling hillside. "Everyone knows Casey," he said, taking a deep breath of cold air. "She practically lives with the basketball team."

"That's true." Virginia couldn't help chuckling.

"And Emily was my next-door neighbor when we lived in that duplex. I told you about that, I think." He cocked his head to look at her.

"Yeah, you did. When you first moved here from Georgia, right?"

He grinned. "Right. Good memory."

Jo stepped up to them. "Virginia, do you know where they're burying Kim?" She stopped and let out a hiccuping sob.

Adam touched her arm. "Why don't you walk with us, Jo?" he offered. "It's over on that hill, I think."

Jo looked back at the church. The pallbearers were carrying the coffin slowly out the side door and heading along a sidewalk toward the grave-yard. "I—I think I'll follow the casket. I'm having a hard time—saying good-bye."

"Are you going to be okay?" Adam asked.

Jo nodded and gave him a quick hug. Then she hurried off toward the procession of family members following the casket.

"You know Jo, too?" Virginia asked.

Adam gave a quick nod. "Remember when I told you that Kim's car broke down?"

"Yeah," Virginia replied, following the stream of people winding up the wintry hillside.

"I took her to our place to use the phone. We were still in the duplex and boy, was it crowded." Adam shook his head ruefully. "Anyway, she called Jo to come get her. We waited and waited, and when it got to be suppertime, Kim stayed for dinner with my family and the Wolfes next door. It was late November and we all joined forces to finish off the Thanksgiving leftovers. Kim was making jokes about turkey soup and turkey loaf and turkey pudding, which really tickled the little kids. She said she was a vegetarian, which she wasn't, and she made a big deal of everything turning out to be turkey, even the salad. Jo finally showed up, and we ended up having a nice evening."

He paused for a minute and Virginia thought, *Maybe the memory's depressing him.*

"I was just thinking," Adam said, "that actually, it's Emily who's the vegetarian. And she really was disgusted by the turkey. She didn't eat a thing."

They were about halfway to the grave site. In the distance, Virginia saw the dark blue awning flapping in the wind over the open pit.

"So," Adam said with a shrug. "That's how I know Jo, Emily, and Kim. But it's weird. I never see them at school."

They were close enough to the grave to hear the minister intoning, "We are here to commit the body of Kim Keller to the earth . . ."

"Come on," Adam said, quickening his steps.

"Wait, I need to tell you—" Virginia said.

Adam put his finger to his lips and hurried toward the grave. "Shhh. The service is starting."

She hadn't had a chance to tell Adam about the note. To warn him. And in a moment they'd be in a crowd of people again and unable to talk. Her skin prickled with anxiety. She had to tell him soon.

Adam found a place on the edge of the crowd and Virginia's heart skipped a beat. He was only a few feet from Alice Monroe. Virginia looked around for Ms. Denson or the police officer. *If I could just see them, I wouldn't feel so nervous.*

The service was mercifully short. As the pastor read some comforting passages from the Bible, Kim's little brother sobbed into his father's shoulder and tears sprang to Virginia's eyes.

She groped in her purse for a tissue. Her chilled fingers touched a crinkly piece of paper. *Wait a second. This isn't a tissue.* She opened the top of her purse a little wider and blinked the tears from her eyes. *That's funny. All I had was in here this morning was my wallet, a comb, and some tissues.*

She swiped at her eyes quickly with the back of her hand. *It's a note.* Someone, she figured must have put it in her purse when she wasn't looking.

The note was on the same computer paper Desperate always used, but this time the message had been written by hand. As Virginia focused her eyes on the angry scrawl of words, a surge of terror shook her body.

That's it. Two strikes and you're out.

chapter 11

"Are you okay?"

The familiar voice seemed to be coming from a long way off. Virginia tilted her head slightly and gazed up into a pair of sea-green eyes.

Adam, with lines of concern engraved on his handsome face, stared down at her as a chill wind breathed against her cheek.

"What?" Virginia looked around. She was no longer at the graveside but farther down the hill, a couple of hundred feet from the crowd at the grave. She and Adam were sitting beside a frozen water fountain in a small grove of trees. "What are we doing down here?"

"You started shaking uncontrollably. I thought you were going to faint, so I carried you down here." Adam touched her cheek and Virginia pulled away quickly, afraid whoever had written the note would be watching.

"Are you all right?" His voice was soft, like a caress. "I understand. A lot of people are overcome with grief at a funeral. It's perfectly natural."

Virginia squeezed her eyes closed, trying to collect her wits. "It's not that, Adam. Here," She opened her hand, revealing the crumpled note. "Look at this."

He stared down at the paper. "What is it?"

"A letter from Desperate. She's after you. After both of us." Virginia took a deep breath. *Calm down. He'll think you're a lunatic.* "Last night she left a note warning me to stay away from you, and since I didn't heed her warning, she sent this threat."

"Whoa." Adam held up one hand. "Back up. Desperate is a person?"

Virginia nodded. "I've been answering the Heart-to-Heart letters for the paper and—"

"You write that column?" he cut in.

"Kim used to do it. But I took over on Friday, when she . . . Anyway, I've been receiving these letters from a girl who's been complaining about a boy who jilted her."

He stared into her eyes. "And?"

"I think that boy is you."

Adam pulled back in alarm. "But that's crazy."

"I think this girl is seriously disturbed," Virginia continued, placing her hand on his arm. "At first her letters were just bitter and angry. Then they quickly turned to actual threats. I connected her words to the bizarre incidents at the newsroom—the matte knife, the sliced-up team picture, and the missing Honor Roll and Science Club article."

"But what does any of that have to do with me?"

"I tried to tell you on the phone. Only two guys at Fairview were in the team photo, the Science Club article, and on the Honor Roll list. You and Skip Parker."

Adam frowned. "So why don't you think it's Skip she's after?"

"Because he's had a steady girlfriend for two years," Virginia replied. "Desperate's hurt is a fresh hurt."

"That's how she signs her letters?" Adam asked, his face paling in the afternoon light. "'Desperate'?"

Virginia nodded. "At first I thought it meant

desperately in love, but now I know it means desperate for revenge."

Adam stood up, his face twitching with exasperation. "But Virginia, I hardly know anybody. I don't see how it could possibly be me. Okay, I admit I'm involved in the three activities you mentioned, but here's the bottom line—I don't have a girlfriend."

"Let me tell you what the letters said exactly. Maybe that will give you a better idea of what I'm talking about. The first one said, 'If you cut me I will bleed. If you hurt me I will die. He hurt me. My heart aches. I am dying. I want him to know my pain.'"

Adam stared at her. "Weird."

"The second note said, 'Dingdong the witch is dead. Now she calls the grave her bed. She did us all a favor. Happy?'"

Adam gasped. "That's horrible! Was she talking about Kim?"

"It was just after we heard the news about her death."

"But why would she think you'd be happy?" Skip asked.

Virginia looked down at the note. "Because Kim and I had an argument Friday morning, which Desperate must have overheard." Virginia could feel her cheeks heating up. "It wasn't a big fight, but I feel awful about it, just awful."

Adam touched her cheek once more, and this time she didn't pull away. She liked his touch. "Were there only two letters?" he asked.

Virginia shook her head. "I made the connection between the strange incidents in the newsroom and the letters when I got the third letter. It said, 'He's disappearing slowly. First his name. Then his face. Soon he'll be gone without a trace.'"

"She's gruesome," Adam said with a shudder.

Virginia nodded. "You see, she eliminates your name by getting rid of any lists or articles that include it. Your face she took care of with a knife." Virginia's stomach knotted as she contemplated the rest of Desperate's plan.

"But I still don't see how you can be so certain it's me she's talking about," Adam said, facing her with his hands on his hips.

Virginia was starting to tremble again. She didn't know if it was from the cold or terror. "Last night, at three-thirty in the morning, I saw someone standing in my front yard. When I woke up, there was a note on my front porch."

"What did it say?"

"'Stay away from him, bitch. Or what happened to Kim will happen to you.'"

"What happened to Kim—" Adam's eyes suddenly grew huge. "Virginia, that means . . ." He put one hand to his head and spun in a circle. "Oh, my God."

Virginia leaned forward. "The police are already involved." She looked over her shoulder toward the graveside. Beside the awning stood two men in dark suits watching the crowd carefully. One of them kept glancing their way. "Just as the funeral was starting, Ms. Denson, who's a counselor for the police department, told me they had declared Kim's death a homicide."

"Homicide." Adam was overwhelmed. He paced back and forth in front of the fountain. "Kim Keller was murdered. That's just impossible. Murder!"

Virginia could barely whisper the next few words. "And we may be next." She thrust the note in front of him once more. "You see what it says—'Two strikes and you're out.'"

"Okay." Adam perched on the fountain's edge beside her. He was definitely agitated, and kept clapping his hands together, trying to think. "Okay, let's say there is someone who's confused—about me. And is trying to get back at me for something I did. Why would she be threatening you?"

"She must have seen us together at Ziggy's," Virginia replied. "Then later she snuck over to my house and left a note warning me to stay away from you."

Adam wrinkled his forehead. "All because we ate some pizza together? This is so bizarre."

"She must have thought we were on a date. You said yourself it was possible." Virginia remembered their phone conversation and how embarrassed she'd felt when Adam had teased her about how some people could interpret a trip to the pizza parlor as a date.

"I did?"

"On the phone. Remember? You said you hadn't dated anyone but me."

He grinned at her. "Oh, yeah. I did. I just meant that some people can take a little thing and—"

"That's it!" Virginia cried. "It's easy to interpret the same event in different ways. Like someone seeing us at the pizza parlor and thinking it was a date. I think some people will believe just about anything. And Desperate truly believes you jilted her."

"Okay." Adam clapped his hands together once more. "We know two things for sure. One, that Desperate is someone who exaggerates everything. And two, that Desperate had to have been at Ziggy's last night."

"And the basketball game on Friday," Virginia added.

"And she must be here now." Adam pointed up at the hill, where the crowd of mourners stood huddled, their backs turned to the fierce north wind.

"Ashes to ashes. Dust to dust." The minister's words drifted down the hill. He then gestured to Dave Ferguson, a senior at Fairview, who was holding a guitar.

"'From a Distance' was one of Kim's favorite songs," Dave told the mourners. "Her parents have requested that I sing it." The plaintive opening chords of Julie Gold's song floated on the wind.

"From a distance the world looks blue and green, and the snowcapped mountains white . . ."

Adam offered his arm to Virginia. "We should go say good-bye."

Virginia looped her arm through his and together they climbed back up the hill.

"It's very scary to think that Desperate is here in this group," Virginia whispered to Adam as they rejoined the mourners around the grave.

He nodded. "She could be standing right next to us."

Suddenly, a blonde girl in the front row turned around, her wide eyes nervously searching the crowd.

"Alice!" Virginia gasped. "Of course."

For a moment their eyes met and Alice seemed to flinch. Then Virginia watched her squeeze between several mourners and bolt down the hill toward the parking lot.

"Come on!" Virginia grabbed Adam's hand. "We have to follow her!"

"Follow who?" Adam shouted as she pulled him down the grassy hill after Alice. Virginia watched Alice climb into an old station wagon and quickly maneuver out of her parking space and into the line leaving the lot.

"Alice Monroe," Virginia explained. "I remember now. She was at the pizza parlor." They jogged to Adam's car, which was hidden behind a thick hedge near the corner of the church. "I'm certain she's Desperate."

"But I don't know anyone named Alice

Monroe," Adam protested as he hopped into his car and started the engine.

"Didn't you recognize that blonde who hurried past us?" Virginia asked, sliding into the passenger seat.

"Yes. She has a locker near mine. But she's a sophomore, isn't she?" Adam nosed his car into the line leaving the parking lot. "I see her in the halls now and then and say hello, but that's it."

"Do you say hello *every* time you see her?" Virginia quizzed him. "And do you always smile?"

"I guess so. But that's because she seems kind of lonely."

"There." Virginia threw her hands in the air. "Don't you see? You were so friendly and charming, she probably thought you liked her."

He shook his head. "Just by saying hello?"

Virginia sighed. "Adam, people can twist signs of friendliness into all sorts of weird things." She didn't want to mention that on Friday even she had gotten confused and thought her neighbor was asking her out for a date. "It happens all the time."

"But we need more than her having a locker near mine to accuse her of being Desperate."

"Yesterday morning I caught her at the Incoming box outside the *Spectator*," Virginia continued. "And I remember seeing her in the parking lot when we arrived at Ziggy's. I even thought at the time maybe she was following you."

Alice's station wagon, which was about ten cars ahead, sped down the main road back into Fairview. Her right-turn indicator went on just before Bush Street.

"She's turning," Virginia said, pointing.

Adam nodded. "I think she's going back to the high school."

"At the funeral, she was sitting close enough to me to slip a note into my bag when everyone was mashed together in the aisle," Virginia noted. "And, let's face it, Adam, she's strange."

Adam let out a sigh of exasperation. "You can't accuse people of murder just because they're a little odd. And besides, anybody could have slipped that note into your purse. The church was packed."

Virginia didn't want to consider any reasons why Alice might not be Desperate. It all fit together too well. She watched Alice's station wagon pull into the school parking lot. Adam was close behind. As they turned onto the asphalt drive, he put his foot on the brakes to slow down.

Thunk!

His foot slammed straight to the floor.

"The brakes!" he gasped. "They're gone!" Adam pumped the pedal frantically, but nothing happened. Virginia held her breath as the car veered straight for the side of the school building. A wall of solid brick loomed in front of them. "Hang on, Ginny!"

Adam twisted the steering wheel violently to the right. Virginia gripped the door handle and her seat belt. With tires screaming, they skidded sideways. At the last second, Adam managed to steer the car away from the school.

Cccrrruuuuunnnnch!

The wheels bounced up over a bike rack and metal screeched against metal beneath the car. Virginia was thrown forward, then back against her seat, but her seat belt held fast. The car finally lurched to a stop, impaled on the bike rack.

They sat for several moments, listening to their hearts beating furiously in their chests. Finally Adam turned to Virginia. "Are you okay?"

"I think so," Virginia answered in a tiny voice. "How about you?"

"I don't know." Adam crunched open his door and peered down at the ground. "I can't believe this. We're high-centered on this bike rack."

Virginia opened the door on her side and looked at the ground, three feet down. On shaky legs, she carefully climbed over the crumpled metal, then stood as far away from the car as she could possibly get. After what had just happened, Virginia feared it might suddenly rock sideways and fall on her.

Adam knelt to peer under the car, and swore. "The brake line's been cut! Someone tried to kill us! Virginia, this is incredible. I thought you were—never mind."

"You thought I was just paranoid, didn't you?"

He blushed.

"Well, now you know I wasn't paranoid *enough*," Virginia said, searching the school grounds. "Alice's car is over there. I'm surprised she's not here watching us suffer."

Adam stood up and brushed the dirt off the knees of his jeans. "Let's go find her." He held out his hand and she grabbed it.

They sprinted across the parking lot and rounded the building toward the Bungalow.

Alice was standing next to the Incoming Heart-to-Heart box. She was crying.

They stopped, then ducked behind some bushes.

"What's she up to?" Adam whispered.

They watched Alice slowly draw a letter from her purse, then lift the hinged lid of the box.

"She's mailing another letter!" Virginia whispered back.

The hinge squeaked as Alice dropped the letter inside, then hurried off toward the parking lot.

"Now we've got her." Virginia lunged for the Incoming Heart-to-Heart box. She reached inside and pulled out a lavender sheet of paper.

"Lavender?" Her breath stuck in her chest, and she slumped against the wall clutching the stationery.

Adam stared at her. "What's wrong? Virginia?"

Virginia held up the letter. "Lavender paper. Handwritten in red ink. It's not Desperate! It's Nobody."

chapter 12

"So Nobody was writing the same kinds of letters as Desperate?" Adam was sitting next to Virginia at her desk in the newsroom. She'd let them into the Bungalow and now they were waiting for the heat to kick in.

"Sort of," Virginia replied. "But hers were the 'poor me' type. You know—'No one likes me.' 'I'm lonely.' Those kind of letters." She shook her head in bewilderment. "I really feel stupid accusing Alice of being Desperate. Some detective I turned out to be."

Adam patted her shoulder. "Don't feel bad. I went along with you."

"I'm sorry about your car." Virginia grimaced as she thought about the Honda, which was completely totaled. "We could've been killed chasing the wrong girl."

"But it's good we came after her. If we'd gone into town with those brakes, we could've caused a terrible accident." He paused, fear flickering in his eyes. "Then Desperate really might have succeeded in killing us both."

Virginia shuddered. "Scary."

"This way, we just creamed the Honda and the bike rack." Adam's eyes twinkled. "I think my parents will understand."

"You're sure?"

"Yeah." He shrugged. "They'll be so relieved we didn't end up dead that they won't even notice the car has no engine."

"It's hard to believe someone cut the brakes while we were at the funeral." Virginia tapped her lips with her finger, thinking. "If it wasn't Alice, who was it? Let's add up the evidence."

"Okay, Sherlock." Adam picked up a pencil from the can on her desk and started jotting notes on a pad of paper. "Desperate was at the funeral. Along with five hundred other people."

"And the basketball game last Friday," Virginia added. "Along with about six hundred other kids."

Adam raised the pen in the air. "*And* Desperate might not have gone to the game. She may have just come here, to the newsroom."

"That's true." Virginia crossed to the hot plate and flicked it on. A hot cup of tea always made her think better. "So it had to be someone who had access to the newsroom."

"Sounds like an inside job," Adam said, drawing a star on the paper.

Virginia frowned. "You mean, someone on the newspaper staff?"

"Was the place broken into?" Adam sat up straight, his face suddenly very serious.

"No." Virginia filled the kettle with water and placed it on the burner.

"Why didn't we think of this before?" He scribbled furiously on the pad. "Could someone have left the door unlocked?"

"Of course." She bit her lip. "Early in the year, we were always forgetting. Ms. Burns got so annoyed with us she threatened to lower our grades if we didn't shape up. But we've been getting better about not leaving the door unlocked."

Adam jumped to his feet. "Okay. So, if someone left the door unlocked, it could've been anybody. But if the door was locked, then only a member of the staff could've gotten in."

"But there's no way to find out," Virginia said, opening the cupboard above the sink and grabbing cups and two tea bags. "Besides, they're my closest friends! We work side by side every day."

Adam gave her a quick smile. "Okay. We'll leave the suspect list open for a moment. You found the second letter waiting for you on Monday morning? Right?"

She nodded. "It was in the Incoming box."

"Let me see the letters."

Virginia retrieved the file with the letters and handed it to Adam. He sat back down at her desk and began to read. "Computer paper. So who on the staff has a computer at home?"

"Casey."

Adam wrinkled his brow. "Well, this doesn't sound like Casey Collier to me, but why don't you call her and ask her about her printer."

"Won't that sound suspicious?" Virginia asked. "I mean, Casey will think I'm acting pretty weird."

Adam narrowed his sea-green eyes at Virginia. "Kim was killed. Our brakes were cut. If we don't get to the bottom of this now, who knows what we'll find waiting for us outside."

"Right." Virginia reached for the phone and punched in Casey's number.

"Colliers," a hoarse voice answered on the second ring. It was Casey, and she sounded like she had definitely been crying.

"Casey? It's Virginia. I—I'm working on the special article about the funeral here at school, and I wondered if you got any pictures today."

"No," Casey replied. "I just couldn't bring myself to start snapping shots during that service. Emily's here and we've been looking through old annuals and remembering Kim. Did you say you were at school?"

"Yes, I came here right from the funeral."

"Geez, Virginia, don't you ever rest? Emily was right. You *are* a compulsive Virgo."

Virginia winced. She decided to get to the point. "Look, Casey, I'm having a problem with our printer here. I was wondering if yours has a sharp enough resolution for some of the layout we need to do."

"Are you kidding?" Casey chuckled. "Mine's an obsolete and incredibly ugly dot matrix. I always use the one at school if I need to print anything that has to be legible."

She shook her head at Adam, who slumped back in his chair.

"Okay, thanks. Just thought I'd ask." Virginia hung up and sighed. "It's not Casey. She has an old dot matrix."

The kettle whistled and Virginia went to make their tea. As she was pouring their cups, she spotted a crumpled gauze Band-Aid resting on the back of the sink.

"Adam," Virginia murmured, staring at the bandage. "Both Jo and Emily were wearing Band-Aids on Monday. Jo said her cat bit her hand and Emily said she cut her hand on a coffee cup. But either one of them could have been lying."

He looked puzzled for a moment, then nodded. "I get it. Whoever sliced the basketball picture could have gashed herself in her fury. Easy to do with those matte knives. That would account for the blood on the picture."

"Right." Virginia was carrying their tea to the desk when the bungalow door creaked open. The wind rustled the loose papers on the workstations.

"Look out," Virginia gasped as hot tea spilled down the front of her dress.

A tall, broad-shouldered figure stepped into the room.

"Sam! You scared us to death!" Virginia cried. "Why were you sneaking in here like that?"

Sam blinked at them in surprise. "I wasn't sneaking. Hey, Adam. What are you doing here?" He looked back and forth from Virginia to Adam, and then his eyes widened. "Oh. I'm sorry, I didn't mean to interrupt. After I left the funeral, I didn't feel like going home alone so I, uh, thought I'd stop by here. Maybe play some Tetris on the computer."

"Sam?" Virginia dabbed at the spilled tea with a rag from the sink. "You wouldn't happen to know if Jo or Emily got a new computer recently, would you?" She tossed the rag in the sink and moved to get her letter file. She handed him one of the letters from Desperate. "This would be the kind of printer it uses."

Sam studied the paper, then looked up at her. "It doesn't matter if they got a new computer or not. This was printed here. See?" He pointed to the top of the page. "It's got this weird glitch. I haven't had time to straighten it out. The second line from the top always prints too light, like it's running out of toner ink."

Virginia stared at the note when he handed it back. "I can't believe I never noticed that before."

She scanned the other letters from Desperate. "The same paper. The same print, except for this last one." She looked up at Adam and murmured sadly, "You're right. It must be someone on the staff."

Adam turned to Sam. "Is there any way to check and see who's been on these computers?"

"Sure. We have a log-on procedure. Anytime one of us uses the unit, it records the time and date, plus their personal user ID." Sam stepped to the computer nearest him and flicked it on. He called up a file that he'd been working on. "See?"

The screen flickered for a few seconds as the computer clicked through its opening sequence. A prompt appeared on the screen that read, "Sam C., Tuesday, Jan. 25, 12:30 P.M."

Adam and Virginia looked at each other. She stood behind Sam, clutching her teacup and peering over his shoulder. Adam moved close beside her. "Sam," Virginia said excitedly. "Could you call up something written last Friday night?"

He pushed some keys, and the screen scrolled toward the information, but when the file came up it was blank. "Nothing."

"What about early Monday morning, before school?" Adam asked. He pressed another series of keys. "Nothing there, either."

"I don't get it," Virginia said, taking a sip of her tea. "Why isn't there a record of this letter? I got it on Monday morning."

"Easy," Sam said, snapping his fingers. "Someone erased it."

Suddenly something bumped against the building, and Virginia jumped. "What was that?"

Adam looked over his shoulder toward the door. "Probably a branch in the wind." He turned back to Sam. "Can you call up any hidden codes that might reveal the network activity?"

Sam grinned at him. "I can do better than that."

Virginia heard another *clunk* and snaked her way between Sam and Adam to check outside. She sniffed the air. An odd smell hovered around the door. "Can you guys smell that?"

Sam, who was typing away furiously, said, "I saw the janitor earlier. Maybe Mr. Robinson finally cleaned the Bungalow. Come here, Ginny." He gestured for her to join him and Adam. "I want you to see what I've done."

Virginia stood at the door a minute longer.

The smell was getting stronger, acrid and bitter, like cleaning solution. It reminded her of the time her parents remodeled the house.

"Can you retrieve the log-on record for the past week?" Adam leaned forward, anxiously watching Sam's screen.

"We're definitely out of luck for Friday and Monday," Sam said. "But I think we can find everything after that. After what happened to my story over the weekend, I installed an automatic backup system that works silently in the background." He pulled open a drawer beneath the computer and pointed to a separate disk drive. "Anything that's been written on our system since Tuesday is right there. But first—" He gave Adam and then Virginia a penetrating look. "You're going to have to tell me what I'm looking for. And why."

Virginia explained the letters from Desperate, the photo, the note in her purse, and their narrow escape in Adam's car. Sam's forehead was deeply lined by the time she finished.

"So you see, Sam," Virginia said, pursing her lips, "I'm afraid it's someone on the *Spectator* staff."

"Someone who saw Ginny and me together at the pizza parlor," Adam added. "And someone who was near enough to Virginia at the funeral to slip a note into her purse."

"So, if you received a note at three-thirty this morning," Sam said thoughtfully, "we can assume the last time she wrote on the machine was last night."

Virginia nodded. "Or very early this morning."

Sam punched some keys, and the lights on the backup system lit up. "Let's go fishing."

Virginia watched commands flow past on the screen and then, wrinkling her nose, went over to the door again. "Adam, come here. Do you know what that smell is?"

He stepped to the door and sniffed. "Smells like someone's doing some painting."

"No, it's not paint," Virginia cried. "I know what it is—it's paint thinner! I wonder why it's so strong right here."

"Mr. Robinson is probably cleaning brushes," Sam said. "He's always painting something that army-surplus pond-scum color."

Virginia and Adam crossed back to the computer. Virginia couldn't shake the feeling that she was a target. It made her want to keep looking over her shoulder.

"Adam?"

"Hmmm?" He was staring at Sam's computer screen.

"If it does come down to Jo or Emily, which one could have possibly thought she dated you?"

Adam scratched his head. "Jo met me the time she came over to pick Kim up at the duplex. She was very funny and we got along great. Later, she interviewed me for that basketball article. I think she might have even asked me out during the interview. But she was only kidding."

"Are you sure?" Virginia narrowed her eyes at him. "If you turned her down she may have taken that as a slight. How did she act at the end of the interview?"

"I don't remember, exactly. I mean, we laughed a lot about the benchwarmer strategy and all. But the interview was here at school. And after she talked to me, she interviewed the starting five on the team." Adam shook his head. "But I don't think it could be Jo. She's so easygoing."

Virginia bit her lip thoughtfully. "Maybe Jo hides a mean streak under that goofball exterior."

"I got it!" Sam threw both hands in the air triumphantly. "Here's Tuesday. Wow. Busy day. Trip. Trip. Sam. Virginia."

"What about the turkey dinner, Adam?"

Virginia prodded as Sam continued his search on the computer. "Kim, Jo, and you were together, right?"

"And Emily," Adam said. "Those first few months, Emily's family and mine were always eating together. It became sort of a . . ."

"Habit?" Virginia asked.

Adam nodded slowly. "But that one night when we were all there, Kim entertained the little kids. She let them try on her jewelry, put makeup on them, everything. They had a blast."

"Tell me again what Jo and Emily were doing," Virginia said.

"Kim was the center of attention while she played with the kids. Jo was mostly in the kitchen, helping Mom and Mrs. Wolfe get the food ready. The only person who didn't seem to have any fun was—"

"Here it is," Sam yelled. "I've got it. Tuesday, eight A.M. And Wednesday, two-thirty A.M."

The name flashing on the screen burned into Virginia's mind. The three of them stared at it for several seconds before they all said it together.

"Emily."

Suddenly the door behind them swung open and banged against the inside wall. All three turned to look in alarm. Virginia sucked in her breath, then grabbed Adam's hand. Emily stood just inside the threshold, her face flushed a bright pink. She held up a silver lighter for Adam to see.

"Kim stole this lighter from your father at the barbecue. I watched her slip it into her pocket." Emily's voice was cold, almost expressionless. "I should have told everyone then, but you wouldn't have cared, would you?"

Adam stiffened.

"She was Miss Perfect, wasn't she?" Emily continued. Her normally cool blue eyes were shining with an unnatural brightness. "But I knew the truth about her. And I never let her forget it."

"Emily, what are you talking about?" Adam asked softly.

Her eyes narrowed. "I wrote Kim letters. Lots of them. I told her that I knew about her little habit of stealing clothes and anything else she could get her hands on."

"It was you in the bungalow Friday morning," Virginia whispered. "You and Kim were having a fight. I heard her shout, 'Stop torturing me.'"

"That's right." Emily's mouth twisted into a sick smile. "But I wouldn't stop. Poor baby."

Virginia pressed her hand to her temple,

which was starting to throb with pain. "You must have followed Kim out of the parking lot. I seem to remember hearing another car."

"I chased her. I told Kim she could run, but she couldn't hide."

"What did you do?" Adam demanded. "Chase her off the road?" The harshness in his voice betrayed his disgust at what Emily was telling them.

Emily smiled. "Oh, no. She did that all by herself. All I needed to do was cover the car with brush so no one would pull her out and save her. My camouflage worked, too."

Virginia covered her mouth in horror. "She was still alive . . . ?"

"Oh, my God." Adam's lips barely moved. "You are sick."

Beside them, Sam rose slowly from his chair and started to inch forward toward Emily.

"It's really all your fault, Adam." Emily shook her hair out of her face and spoke in a nonchalant voice. "You invited Kim to our house for dinner."

"Emily," Adam said, trying to keep his voice steady. "You know I picked Kim up after her car broke down. That's all. I just gave her a ride. There wasn't anything between us."

"You didn't have to bring her to our house." Emily's face formed an ugly grimace. "To our secret garden."

"She needed to call Jo for help." Adam met her gaze, trying to hold it. "You remember. She called Jo."

"But it was *our* secret garden," Emily said softly, taking a step toward him. "How could you, Adam? How could you let her come into the garden?"

Emily looked feverish. Her cheeks were blazing red and little beads of sweat covered her brow.

"Garden?" Virginia murmured to Adam.

"There was an old-fashioned greenhouse behind the duplex," Adam explained, never taking his eyes off Emily. "Emily took it over as her own, planting all sorts of beautiful flowers. Sometimes, when I was baby-sitting, she'd invite the kids and me inside. They called it the Secret Garden, like in the storybook."

"And you picked a rose and gave it to me," Emily whispered. "I pressed it, to keep forever."

Adam shook his head. "Emily, I didn't pick that rose. It had fallen off the bush onto the greenhouse floor. All I did was pick it up and hand it to you."

"No!" Emily shouted. "You picked it for me!" Her breathing was shallow and fast, and perspiration now covered her face like a mist. "Then you brought Kim into our garden and it never was the same. She took you away from me."

"No she didn't." Adam's voice shook with frustration. "My family bought a house and we had to move. The duplex was only temporary. You knew that."

Virginia sniffed again. The acrid smell was stronger than ever, wafting in through the open door. She looked down at Emily's feet and noticed a dark patch of liquid spreading into the room. Paint thinner! Emily must have been pouring the flammable fluid around the sides of the Bungalow. One false move and the entire building would go up in flames.

"Kim thought she would take those letters I wrote her to the police," Emily continued. "But she didn't make it, did she?" Emily shook her head. "I reached into the car and plucked those letters right out of her backseat. It was hard, too, with all of that broken glass."

"That's how you cut your hand," Virginia murmured.

Emily gazed down at the bandage on her

hand. "It didn't even hurt." She looked confused for a minute, then settled her gaze back on Adam. He moved closer to Virginia. "I burned them, you know. Just like I'm going to burn the other letters I wrote."

Emily flicked on the lighter, and a pillar of flame shot into the air. She snatched up a piece of paper from the nearest desk and lit one end. The orange light distorted her features into an ugly mask of pain and hate. She thrust the paper torch toward Adam. "The letters will be gone. And so will you."

"Now!" Adam shouted. Sam hurled himself across the room, tackling Emily and throwing her roughly to the floor. The burning paper flew out of her hand and Adam lunged to catch it. It slipped off his fingertips and fluttered down onto the dark pool of paint thinner.

Whooooosh!

A wall of flames roared into the doorway.

"Sam, roll!" Virginia shouted. Sam clutched Emily and rolled away from the door before their clothes could catch on fire.

"Try the windows," Adam shouted, running for the long row against the east wall. But as he grabbed the sill a new curtain of flames flared up in front of him.

"It's already circled the building," Virginia shouted. "We're trapped!"

Thick, billowing clouds of black smoke poured into the room, blinding them. Virginia felt the acrid smoke sear into her lungs.

"Get down," Adam rasped, fighting his way through the thick smoke to Virginia and Sam. "Stay close to the floor."

Virginia covered her mouth with her hand. "What should we do?"

"We have to get out," Sam said, pulling Emily into the center of the room. She'd bumped her head on the file cabinet and was barely conscious.

"What about the back door?" Adam coughed.

Sam shook his head. "There isn't one. Windows—we're supposed to use the windows."

They squinted into the black smoke, but could see nothing except curling orange flames circling the building.

Virginia looked up, her eyes burning. "Up there," she said, pointing to a hinged ceiling panel. "Let's try the roof."

The roar of the fire grew louder, and Virginia felt the heat under the floor through her shoes. Adam pulled Virginia's desk toward them, positioning it beneath the roof access, then climbed onto it. He was barely tall enough to reach the panel. "Virginia, hurry."

Virginia climbed up on the desk as Adam punched at the ceiling panel to open it. The flames roared along all four walls. In the back of the newsroom, a window exploded.

"Quick, Sam," Adam yelled. "Get on the desk. Now."

Sam propped Emily up, and Adam and Virginia pulled her onto the desk. Then Sam hopped up beside them.

"Sam, you go first," Adam ordered, "and I'll hand Emily up to you."

Adam boosted Sam up through the hole in the roof, then reached for Emily and struggled to lift her above his head. Virginia helped, straining her arms to lift the limp weight of the barely conscious girl toward Sam, who reached down to grasp her arms and finally dragged her through.

"Got her," Sam shouted. "You're next, Virginia. Come on."

Virginia raised her arms as Adam grabbed her around the legs. In one fluid movement, he lifted her up and Sam pulled her through the roof. Wind blew into her face and cold air poured into her aching lungs.

Sam leaned over the hole, his back muscles straining. "Come on, man. Jump up—I'll pull you through."

Virginia looked over at Emily, who lay slumped on the roof like a rag doll. Beneath them, the windows were bursting from the heat one by one, rocking the frail structure with each explosion.

"Adam, please hurry," Virginia screamed.

"I can't!" Adam started to cough. "I can't get high enough. I'll have to get a chair."

Sam pulled away from the hole in the roof and wiped the sweat from his face. He took a few deep breaths of fresh air and leaned back in again.

Virginia gripped his arm. "Sam?"

"He'll make it," Sam replied. "Come on, Adam!"

Adam's hand shot through, and Sam yanked with all his might just as another explosion shook the building. The shingles on the roof were now unbearably hot.

"Thanks." Adam stood up on shaky legs, trying to peer through the smoke. "Come on, we've got to get off this roof. Now."

"Over here." Virginia gestured toward the

side of the roof where the flames seemed less intense. She squeezed her eyes shut, frantically trying to remember if there was pavement or grass below.

Adam scooped up Emily, who had begun to sob, and slid toward the edge of the roof. Sam was right beside him,

"It looks like a long way down," Virginia groaned, peering at the ground. Behind her, a burst of flame shot through the center of the roof. They had a few seconds at the most before the whole thing would collapse.

"Can you jump holding Emily, buddy?" Sam asked.

Adam nodded quickly. "I'll make it." He turned to look at Virginia. "I wish we had more time," he whispered.

She touched his hair. "I do, too, Adam."

He nodded, then readjusted his hold on Emily. In the distance they could hear the wail of fire engines.

Sam took Virginia's hand. "Remember, jump as far away from the building as possible."

Virginia gulped and nodded.

"On the count of three," Sam bellowed. "One, two . . ."

Virginia shut her eyes and, mustering every ounce of strength she could, hurled herself into the smoke.

"THREE!"

chapter 13

The Moon lights the way at night for Virgos who have been lost. Your natural leadership ability is rewarded—and your love life isn't suffering either.

Dear Readers,

A great tragedy has happened in our community. We have lost a valued friend. We shall miss Kim and never forget her winning smile and wonderful sense of humor. But we also must remember the lesson this tragedy has taught us. If you have a problem that you can't handle—talk to someone.

We all have had bouts of loneliness and depression. Feelings that we are unloved and that the whole world is against us. But those feelings are temporary and we must not give in to them. If we find that they are ruling our life, then we should find a trusted friend, relative, or counselor to help us.

Emily Wolfe was filled with feelings she couldn't handle alone. And because of that, Kim Keller is gone. If Kim, who had her own dark secrets, could have talked to someone, maybe things would have turned out differently.

The Heart-to-Heart column will now be handled by a professional. Someone who understands more fully the confusing feelings we all can have. Don't be afraid to write anything you feel to her. You will always get careful, honest replies.

Thank you for your support through these difficult times. My heart is always with you.

Virginia Wells,
Editor

Virginia hit print on the new computer that had been set up in the high school garage. It had been nearly three weeks since the fire had burnt the Bungalow to the ground. Three weeks since they had all taken their giant leap.

The temporary home for the *Spectator* wasn't very fancy, but it provided a place for the newspaper staff to get the paper together until a new permanent space could be built.

And right now it felt cozy. Virginia glanced up at Adam, who stood beside her. He leaned heavily on his right leg, since his left one was encased in a walking cast.

"Relieved?" he asked, placing his hand on her shoulder.

"Totally. I'm so glad to be out of the lonely-hearts business and back writing news."

"And you don't feel bad about Sam getting the job as editor?"

Virginia stood up, grabbing her sweater from the back of the chair. "I have to confess, I did at first, but now that I'm used to the idea, I think Sam's the perfect choice. He's level-headed, can definitely handle a crisis, and he's just an all-around great guy."

"Let's just hope his experience isn't as much of a roller-coaster ride as yours," Adam said, looping his hand through her arm.

"Yeah," Virginia chuckled. "I wouldn't want to wish that on anyone."

They walked slowly toward the door, with Adam leaning heavily on his cane.

"How's the leg?" she asked, holding the door for him.

"The doctor said I have to keep it in this walking cast for four more weeks, and then I'm free."

"Four more weeks?" Virginia quickly did some mental calculation. "By that time basketball season will be over."

"Awwwww! Too bad," Adam said with a mock frown. "I guess I'll just have to go out for baseball."

Virginia locked the garage door and they started to walk toward the main school building. As they passed the burnt pit where the Bungalow used to stand, she sighed. "We really were lucky. That roof lasted about two seconds after we jumped."

Virginia was still having nightmares about falling into the flames. But the doctor who had bandaged the gash on her leg and wrapped her sprained ankle had promised the dreams would fade in time.

"It's amazing that no one got seriously hurt," Adam said, shaking his head. "Sam's knees and hands got scraped up, you hurt your ankle and leg, but that's it. And if I hadn't been holding Emily, I wouldn't have broken my leg."

"Emily." Just the mention of her name made Virginia shudder. "I've known her since we were in elementary school. She was always a little quiet and different, but never in a million years would I have imagined that she could be so disturbed."

Adam led Virginia away from the charred piece of ground and toward the school building. "I'm just glad Emily's in the hospital where she can't hurt anybody anymore."

"Until the trial," Virginia said. "That will probably be a painful process for everyone involved."

"Let's not think about that now." Adam threw open the big metal door to the school. "For now let's just enjoy the day and the fact that we're alive."

Virginia smiled. "That's what my horoscope in the *Spectator* told me to do. It said, 'Venus and the Moon make for a brightly colored nightlife. Look up, and you'll see them spelling out romance like a celestial skywriter.'"

"Good horoscope." Adam nodded approvingly. "Who's writing them these days?"

"Trip," Virginia giggled. "I know—Mr. Skeptic. But the King of Sarcasm has really thrown himself into it. And he's good. Or at least, I like what I read."

"Yes, especially the part about making magic." Adam flashed her his lopsided grin and Virginia felt a familiar sizzle of joy skip through her.

They headed down the hall toward the lunchroom, friends greeting both of them along the way. Just before they reached the crowded cafeteria, Adam ducked into a tiny alcove between two sets of lockers, pulling her in with him.

"I have something I've been wanting to ask you

since the day we met," he whispered. "But people and events seemed to conspire against me."

Virginia tilted her chin up to gaze into his eyes. *How can anyone be so handsome?* "Yes?" she whispered back. "What is it?"

"I wonder if you'd care to join me Friday night for a pizza at Ziggy's." He slipped his arm around her waist. "And a movie."

"Is this an official date?" she murmured, as he slowly drew her toward him.

His lips pressed against hers in a kiss. "The first, I hope, of many."